FINAL FANTASY.VII
ON THE WAY TO A SMILE

KAZUSHIGE NOJIMA

CLOUD

TIFA

BARRET & MARLENE

VINCENT

RUFUS, RUDE & RENO

SEPHIROTH

FINAL FANTASY. VII

ON THE WAY TO A SMILE

FINAL FANTASY. VII
ON THE WAY TO A SMILE

KAZUSHIGE NOJIMA

New York

FINAL FANTASY. VII
ON THE WAY TO A SMILE

KAZUSHIGE NOJIMA

Translation by Melissa Tanaka
Editorial Supervision by SQUARE ENIX CO., LTD.

FINAL FANTASY VII On the Way to a Smile
©2009 Kazushige Nojima / SQUARE ENIX CO., LTD.
©1997, 2004–2009 SQUARE ENIX CO., LTD. All Rights Reserved.
CHARACTER DESIGN: TETSUYA NOMURA
First published in Japan in 2009 by SQUARE ENIX CO., LTD. English translation rights arranged with SQUARE ENIX CO., LTD. and Yen Press, LLC through Tuttle-Mori Agency, Inc.

English translation © 2018 by SQUARE ENIX CO., LTD.

Yen On
1290 Avenue of the Americas
New York, NY 10104

Visit us at yenpress.com ✦ facebook.com/yenpress ✦ twitter.com/yenpress ✦ yenpress.tumblr.com ✦ instagram.com/yenpress

First Yen On Edition: October 2018

Yen On is an imprint of Yen Press, LLC.
The Yen On name and logo are trademarks of Yen Press, LLC.

Library of Congress Cataloging-in-Publication Data
Names: Nojima, Kazushige, 1964– author. | Tanaka, Melissa, translator.
Title: Final Fantasy VII : on the way to a smile / Kazushige Nojima ; translation by Melissa Tanaka.
Other titles: Final Fantasy VII. English | Final fantasy.
Description: First Yen On edition. | New York, NY : Yen On, October 2018.
Identifiers: LCCN 2018015073 | ISBN 9781975382353 (pbk.)
Subjects: CYAC: Fantasy games—Fiction. | Magic—Fiction. | Science fiction.
Classification: LCC PZ7.1.N635 Fi 2018 | DDC [Fic]—dc23
LC record available at https://lccn.loc.gov/2018015073

ISBN: 978-1-9753-8235-3

10 9 8 7 6 5 4

LSC-C

Printed in the United States of America

CONTENTS

EPISODE: DENZEL   001

LIFESTREAM: Black I   030

EPISODE: TIFA   031

LIFESTREAM: White I   052

EPISODE: BARRET   053

LIFESTREAM: Black II   072

EPISODE: NANAKI   073

LIFESTREAM: White II   100

EPISODE: YUFFIE   101

LIFESTREAM: Black III   128

EPISODE: SHINRA   131

LIFESTREAM: White III   184

FINAL FANTASY. VII

EPISODE: DENZEL

ON THE WAY TO A SMILE

There were two distinct cityscapes in Midgar. The upper city was built high in the air atop the Plate, which in turn was supported by an array of massive pillars. Below were the slums, where folk lived chaotic but hardy lives in the permanent shadow of the steel structure above. Every resident of Midgar, be they rich or poor, bathed in sunlight or cast in shadow, believed that this amazing city, built by the mighty Shinra Electric Power Company, would be a sight that endured forever.

That is, until four years ago, when the Lifestream started to flow and nearly brought Midgar crashing to the ground. The people grabbed what they could of their belongings and tried to flee, but they found they couldn't bring themselves to go very far from the steel metropolis. Perhaps they thought if they stayed close to its imposing skyline, they could hold on to their dreams of a better future. Eventually, a town sprang up right beside Midgar. They called it Edge.

The main road of Edge began at the boundary between Sectors Three and Four of Midgar and stretched due east. The new settlement sprawled to the north and south of it. From a distance, it looked like a splendid town, but most of the buildings were thrown together from scrap recovered from Midgar. Edge smelled of iron and rust.

Johnny wore his hair slicked back in a pompadour, an unusual style for a young man in those days. He ran a café alongside the main road, a no-frills sort of place that consisted of tables and chairs set out on the empty lot and a stall where he cooked up his basic fare. He called it Johnny's Heaven, by way of homage to Seventh Heaven, a diner and bar he used to frequent in Midgar's Sector Seven slums. He'd had a thing for the pretty bartender there, a girl named Tifa.

That bar had been buried when the Sector Seven section collapsed, but when Edge appeared, Tifa had opened a new Seventh Heaven right here in the new town. At the time, Johnny had been just another one of the displaced young men with vague ambition but no idea what to do next. When he saw Tifa's strength and initiative in the face of disaster, he was inspired. The one-time object of his unrequited crush became a role model. A mentor, even. *I want to live my life the way she does*, he'd thought. *How do I do that? Easy answer is, I'll open a place, too.*

That was the start of Johnny's Heaven, and every customer was subjected again and again to the tale of Johnny Reborn.

Of course, when they heard the story of Tifa, they had to go visit Seventh Heaven and see the inspirational barkeep with their own eyes. Soon enough, they ended up as regulars there, and few of them bothered to return to Johnny's humble stall. Suddenly, Johnny found himself waiting day after day for even one customer who'd be willing to listen to his tale of love and redemption.

Then someone did. It was just a kid, though. *What's this little kid doing out by himself? Oh-ho, if it ain't Denzel!*

This was no ordinary customer. Denzel lived with Tifa, Johnny's unknowing mentor and the object of his affections. *Gotta go all out on this one!*

"Come in! Make yourself at home, Denzel!" he said, bobbing his head and gesturing grandly toward an empty chair.

But Denzel barely glanced in his direction before taking a seat at the table farthest from the stall.

"You can sit closer if you want, kid!"

"No. I'm meeting someone."

Meeting someone? What, like you're on a date at your age? Johnny thought. *Okay, okay. That's good. I'll take good care of you both. Everything on the house for my special customer.*

"A date, huh? Go get her, kiddo!"

"Coffee."

Ticked off? Nah. Probably just shy.

"If you get stuck for things to talk about, just call me over. I've got some great icebreakers. Works great with the ladies. Heck, if you want, I can—"

Suddenly, Denzel jumped to his feet. *Shit, maybe I did piss him off.*

Johnny peered at Denzel, but the kid was looking toward the entrance, where a narrow-faced man in a dark suit now stood.

"We're open," Johnny managed to say without looking him in the eye. It was Reeve, former Shinra bigwig, now the leader of the WRO. He'd never seen the man in the flesh before, but folk whispered that the stench of death clung to him. *What's a guy like that doing at my place?*

Reeve warily scanned the environment as he went to Denzel's table and sat down. Then Johnny figured it out.

Denzel's being scouted for the WRO! Reeve's trying to lure him into signing up. I can't let that happen! If that goes down in my place, I'll lose any chance I ever had with Tifa. He glared at Reeve.

In return, Reeve gave him a placid smile. "A coffee, if you wouldn't mind." *Damn. Dude's got dignity to spare.*

"Sure," Johnny replied, standing ramrod straight. He scurried back to the stall. *Sheesh. He's a real badass, this one.*

If Johnny was surprised, Denzel was dumbstruck that the head of the WRO himself had come to talk to him. He stood there, unable even to muster a greeting.

"Have a seat."

Reeve's voice broke the spell, and Denzel hastily sat down.

"Now, Denzel, I don't have a lot of time, so I'll get right to the point," Reeve began in a measured tone. "You should know first of all that our organization isn't like it used to be. The days of welcoming anyone who was willing to join are long gone. If you want to help in the reconstruction, talk to your local district officer. The WRO is a military institution now."

"Yes, sir. I know it'll be dangerous."

"Do you? So tell me about yourself, kid. What's your background?"

"My background? I don't— I mean, I'm only ten…"

"I'm aware. But even ten-year-olds come from somewhere."

*   *

Denzel was the only child born to Abel, a workaholic employed by the Shinra Electric Power Company's Third Operations Division, and Chloe, a sociable woman who ran a clean, organized home. The three of them lived in company-provided housing in Midgar's Sector Seven.

Born and raised in a poor backwoods village, Abel was more than happy with his life in upper Midgar. However, he believed a man always needed goals, and his had been to live in the coveted Shinra executive housing area. It was a goal he realized a short time before Denzel's seventh birthday, when he earned a promotion to division chief, the position for which benefits included a house in the Sector Five enclave.

Upon hearing the news, Chloe and Denzel prepared a celebration. The proud dad came home to a feast and decorations handmade by Denzel himself. It was a lively dinner, and in high spirits, Denzel's father cracked jokes and told stories about his life.

"Denzel, always remember you're a lucky young boy. If you were born down in the slums, you'd have to eat rats instead of chicken."

"They don't have chicken in the slums?"

"I suppose they might, but no one can afford it. They have to catch rodents instead. Spear them with a stick. Big black rats."

"Ew, gross!"

"Actually, I think they taste just fine," said Abel, patting his stomach and winking at Chloe.

"What about you, Denzel? How do you like them?" Chloe pointed to Denzel's plate.

Denzel looked suspiciously at his parents and then at his plate. His dad was looking away and trying not to laugh. Denzel remembered what his father liked to say: *There's no point to a life without laughter.* They were playing tricks on him again.

"Mom! Dad! Stop with the stupid jokes already!"

*   *

"So your parents would tease you."

"They just liked to joke around, that's all. I mean, I thought it was funny, too."

"For the record, to the best of my knowledge, they didn't eat any rats in the slums. I doubt they were edible, to be frank, and really, the slums weren't as bad as many topsiders believed—"

"Yes, I know. I figured that out myself."

"Oh? How so?"

"...It's a long story."

*   *

Denzel was home alone when the phone rang. It was Abel.

"Where's your mother?!" he demanded.

NANAKI & CAIT SITH

YUFFIE

"She went shopping."

"Tell her to call me right away when she gets home. No, never mind, I'll just come myself."

Denzel could tell there was trouble of some kind. It made him nervous, and then he couldn't concentrate on anything, so he watched TV while he waited for Mom to come home. The news was showing the ruins of Mako Reactor One. Some group called Avalanche had blown it up.

That must be why Dad's cranky. He must be really busy with this disaster. He's not mad at Mom or me.

An hour later, Abel arrived home.

"Where is she?"

"She's not back yet."

"Then we're going to find her." Abel was already out the door again, with Denzel scurrying after him. They went to the market and spotted Chloe soon enough, chatting with the butcher.

Abel told Denzel to stay put and marched over to the butcher's stall. He grabbed his wife by the wrist without a word and dragged her back.

Denzel felt his heart skip a beat at the fear in his mother's voice when she protested.

"Let me *go*! What's gotten into you?"

Abel looked from side to side and whispered, "They're going to destroy Sector Seven. We have to leave for Sector Five right now. We can go to the new house."

"Destroy it?"

"Those lunatics who blew up the reactor. They're targeting Sector Seven next."

Denzel studied his mother's expression. She wasn't laughing.

"Is this for real?" He clutched at his parents' hands. "Hey, c'mon. We gotta go."

But neither of them moved.

"We can't just run off and save ourselves. We have to warn our neighbors, our friends!"

"There's no time, Chloe. And this is top-secret company intelligence. I only just got promoted, and I'm already breaking the rules…"

Chloe shook her head furiously and turned to Denzel. "You go with your father. And I'll come find you soon. It'll be okay."

She squeezed his hand once before letting go, and then she ran off.

"No!" Abel began to chase after her, but he gave up after a few steps.

Denzel's chest felt tight as he looked up at his father's stricken face. *He wants to go after her*, he thought. *But he's got to look after me…*

"Come on, Denzel. We're going to Sector Five."

"But what about Mom?!"

"She'll be okay. She's just being the family conscience."

A man in his early twenties was dragging a heavy suitcase along the road dividing Sectors Six and Seven. His tie was askew, his jacket unbuttoned, and he wore an expression of dogged desperation. He was clearly in a hurry.

"Arkham!" Abel called out to him.

Hearing his name, the man looked up and spotted Abel. "Chief, you're still here? The Turks have already deployed. They must have planted the explosives by now. I know a guy from the maintenance section who prepped their vehicles."

Having heard his father talk about Shinra his entire life, Denzel knew a lot about the company's organization. Such as the fact that the Turks were the ones who did the company's dirty work.

Explosives? The Turks are going to blow something up? But does that mean the Turks are also Avalanche? He was staring at the ground, trying to make sense of the grown-ups' exchange, when he felt his father's gaze and looked up.

"Would you take my boy over to Sector Five? I'd consider it a personal favor," Abel said, still looking at his son.

"No!" Denzel shouted.

"I'll go and get your mother. You go along with Mr. Arkham here."

"I wanna stay with you!"

"Can I count on you, Arkham?"

"Of course, sir."

"Number thirty-eight in the Sector Five enclave. Here's the key. My son will look after it. Right?" Abel took a key from the inside pocket of his jacket and pressed it into Denzel's hand.

"Dad—"

"I bought us a new big-screen TV. You can watch your shows while you wait for us." He ruffled Denzel's hair a little too hard and gave him a shove toward the Arkham guy. Then he took off sprinting into Sector Seven.

The man caught Denzel as the boy stumbled. "All right, kid, let's go. Name's Arkham. I work for your dad. Nice to meet you."

Denzel squirmed and tried to run after Abel, but Arkham held him fast. "I know how you feel. But your dad told me to take you home, and that's exactly what I'm gonna do. So let's just get you to Sector Five, and after that, it's up to you. Okay?"

The new house, one in a long row of cookie-cutter look-alikes, was empty save for a large box containing the new TV set.

Arkham wrestled the TV out of the packaging and plugged it in. The two of them sat on the floor watching the news, which was still showing footage of the blown-up Reactor One. Denzel tried to think of how to get this stranger to leave.

"I'm hungry," he said.

"All right. I'll go get you something."

And then the whole house shook. From somewhere far off, they could hear a mighty crash, and then the scream of twisting metal.

"Stay here," Arkham ordered, and then he rushed outside.

Denzel moved to the door, too, but then the voice on the television brought him up short. *"Breaking news!"*

Now the screen was showing a falling city.

It took a minute before Denzel realized he was looking at a huge section of the Plate collapsing earthward into the slums below. Sector Seven, where he had just been with his parents a few hours ago. The scene changed, and the anchor said, *"You are now looking at live footage from Sector Seven."*

There was nothing there. Sector Seven was gone. Denzel tore out of the house.

The city was in chaos. People were running in all directions, screaming that Sector Five could be next. He darted between legs, desperately push-ing through the crowd.

Eventually, out of breath, he reached the edge of Sector Six, but soldiers had already put up roadblocks across the entrances. He peered through the barricades, trying to see where Sector Seven was—but there was nothing. Just empty space. As if it had never been there at all.

Beyond the gap, in the distance, he could just about make out Sector Eight. Its edge was a jagged wound of dangling cables and twisted steel beams.

"Hey, kid. You shouldn't be out here. Where do you live?" said one of the soldiers.

Denzel pointed at the empty space.

"Damn. Sorry to hear that, kid," said the soldier, not unkindly. "Know where your folks are at?"

Denzel pointed again, to the same place.

The guard heaved a sigh. "This is Avalanche's doing. Don't you forget that. When you grow up, you can pay them back," the soldier said, as if to encourage the boy. The soldier put his arm on Denzel's shoulder, turned him back toward Sector Six, and gave him a light push on the back. "You'd best get going now."

In a daze, Denzel started walking. Around him, the rubberneckers and survivors spoke in fear and wonder.

What are they going to blow up next?

Dad!

Is it safe here?

Mom!

Avalanche isn't getting away with this!

What is Shinra doing?!

Dad!

Mom, where are you?

He tuned out the voices, all but one pathetic child's voice that seemed to constantly follow him. Eventually, he realized it was his own, and he stopped, unable to take another step. Then the tears came.

*   *

"Is it true that Shinra did it?"

"Yes." Reeve looked away, as if he'd made up his mind not to show any emotion whatsoever. "You can hate me for it. Get revenge, if you want."

Denzel shook his head.

*   *

Denzel woke up the next day in the new house in Sector Five on a mattress that hadn't been there yesterday. Next to him, he found a note and a pastry.

I'm at work. I'll come to check in on you in a bit. Don't go too far, okay? Everyone's pretty riled up, so it isn't safe outside. It wasn't easy to find you last night, and it wasn't easy carrying you all the way back. —Arkham

P.S. I borrowed the mattress from next door. Make sure you return it.

The TV news was showing footage of the Sector Seven collapse over and over again. The reporters kept rereading the press release from the Shinra Electric Power Company that said Midgar was safe now. But how could anything ever be safe for him, if his parents were dead? It didn't make any sense.

They keep saying it's safe. So does everyone live happily ever after? Do I?

He picked up the pastry, but just before he bit into it, he noticed it was a little crushed, and the cream inside was leaking out. It made him angry. He hurled it at the TV with all his might and stormed outside.

Despite what Arkham had said, the streets were calm. Denzel could see the Shinra Building towering over the center of Midgar. *Dad could still be alive. He and Mom could've gone to the office. I bet he's just really busy, dealing with all the mess. These are all Shinra houses. I bet someone here knows Dad. I hate talking to grown-ups I don't know, but I guess I've gotta suck it up and ask.*

He went to the first door on the right and rang the bell. No answer. Just in case, he tried opening the door.

It was unlocked. He poked his head in.

"Hello?" He waited for a bit, but the house was silent. Maybe Arkham took the mattress from this house. Wasn't borrowing without asking the same as stealing?

He tried the house on the left. Then the ones across the street, then the ones farther up the street. They were all empty. He began ringing bells on the next street over. A lot of houses had notes posted on their front doors to say that the people who lived there were temporarily leaving town. Often, there was a contact number, too.

The whole neighborhood was deserted. And Denzel knew in his heart that his parents weren't at work. They would have come to find him by now. Even if his father couldn't get away, his mother somehow would have made it here.

He walked on, hope surging suddenly then fading away again, until he realized he was completely lost. He couldn't remember the way he'd come. He started to cry, more out of frustration than fear.

He plunked himself down on the sidewalk but jumped up quickly when he realized he'd sat on something hard. It was a toy Shinra airship. *Some kid must've dropped it.*

Denzel picked it up and threw it as hard as he could. "I hate *everyone*!"

The crash of a window shattering echoed down the street, followed by a woman shouting. "Who's there? Who did that?"

Before Denzel realized what was happening, an ancient-looking woman burst out of the house with the smashed window. Actually, maybe she wasn't that ancient, but he was just a kid. How was he supposed to tell?

"Did you just throw this?" With a scowl, she thrust the airship in Denzel's direction.

He nodded dumbly.

"Now, why—?" She cut herself off midsentence. "Are you crying?"

Denzel shook his head in denial, but he couldn't hide his tears.

"Where do you live?"

He didn't know how to answer that, and that only made him angry at himself. He cried harder.

"Well, child. I can't leave you here like this. I suppose you'd best come in."

Ruvie's house had a sweet, cozy feel to it that was quite different from that of his parents' house. There were tiny floral patterns on the wallpaper and the sofa and fake but cheerful flowers in a vase. Denzel sat perched on the edge of the sofa, watching Ruvie warily as she struggled to cover the broken window with a piece of tarp.

"I'm sorry."

"If these were more normal times, I'd have grabbed you by the scruff of your neck and hauled you straight to your folks and given you an earful along the way."

"My mom and dad, they—"

"Don't tell me they skipped town and left you behind."

"They were in Sector Seven."

Ruvie froze. Then she left the window, sat down next to Denzel, and wrapped her arms around him.

When he had cried himself out, she said she would take him outside. "Come on, let's see if we can't find that house of yours."

Ruvie held his hand as they walked. Denzel hadn't held hands with anyone since he turned six. It just wasn't what big kids did. But right now, he didn't care about being a big kid.

The Shinra employees in this neighborhood were bunking at headquarters while their families had fled to Junon or Costa del Sol, according to Ruvie. But she'd stayed behind because, as she explained it, *If you're going to be alone no matter where you go, you might as well be in your own home.*

Eventually, the two of them found Denzel's house.

"Thank you. I'm sorry about your window."

Ruvie only nodded and walked Denzel up to the door, peering inside as he opened it.

"Now, look at that. Empty as a cell. What are you gonna do with yourself in here? Come along, Denzel. I think you need to stay with me for a while."

So Denzel ended up living with Ruvie.

After the explosion at Mako Reactor One, she had stocked up on essentials, anticipating tough times ahead. The shed in her backyard was full of canned food.

"Forewarned is forearmed—isn't that what they say?"

She kept her days full with cleaning and yard work, cooking, and sewing. Denzel helped with everything but the sewing. She would read before going to bed, working through heavy, challenging books.

Denzel asked if they were any good. "Not a bit," Ruvie replied. They were her son's, she explained. For more than five years she had been reading them, trying to understand what her son did for a living. *But I'm no wiser than when I started. All they do is put me to sleep.* She had laughed as she told him.

Ruvie did loan him an illustrated guide to monsters, telling him it would prove useful. That book was her son's, too. He'd read it when he was about Denzel's age. It had full-color pictures of the monsters and descriptions for each one. Every page had the same advice—if you see one of these, run away fast and tell an adult.

If I meet a monster now, I guess I can tell Ruvie. But she doesn't look like she can fight much. I'd probably have to do the fighting for us. But could I beat a monster? Probably not.

I'm useless, Denzel thought. *That's why my parents went to Sector Seven without me.*

*   *

The day was getting warmer, and Denzel was sweating.

"Gracious me, it's hot. How about bringing some water over here?" Reeve said to Johnny.

Denzel took out a handkerchief to wipe his brow.

"Cute handkerchief," Reeve remarked. "Did a girl give it to you?"

"Sort of." Denzel stared down at the fabric.

*   *

One morning when he came down for breakfast, Ruvie held up a collared shirt and said, "Here, I made this for you. It's the only fabric I had." The shirt was white and decorated with little pink flowers. In another time, Denzel would have refused to wear it, but now, he put it on, delighted.

"And I made these with the scraps. Here you go." She offered him a pile of handkerchiefs with the same pattern as the shirt. There must have been quite a lot of extra fabric, judging by how many she'd made. Denzel took just one, folded it carefully, and put it in his pocket.

"One other thing…" The smile had left Ruvie's face. "I'm not sure how to put this…"

A sudden chill ran through Denzel. He imagined the worst thing she could say. *It's time for you to leave.* The very idea made him shake.

"Why don't we go outside?" Ruvie went out the back door to the yard.

Denzel hesitated, then followed, stepping across the well-packed soil to stand beside her. Ruvie was looking up at the sky.

He followed her gaze and saw the thing above them—a big black smudge, a truly ominous sight. You weren't supposed to see black in the sky during the day. Only blue or white. Anything else was wrong, and frightening.

"They're calling it 'Meteor.' It's small now, but it's going to get a whole lot bigger. Then it'll hit our planet and wipe us out. Wipe out everything." Ruvie took two cans from the shed and handed them to Denzel. "How are we supposed to prepare for something like that, for crying out loud?"

That day, she didn't do any cleaning or sewing. She spent the whole time sitting on the sofa, thinking.

She did try to make a few phone calls, several times throughout the day. But whoever she was calling, they weren't picking up. *Maybe she's trying to call her son*, Denzel thought as he cleaned the house inside and out.

He couldn't really imagine what would happen when Meteor hit. And anyway, he had another question on his mind. He just didn't know how to bring it up.

Finally, when it got dark, Ruvie started cleaning, too, as if waking from a reverie. "You're not doing it right, Denzel. Haven't you been watching how I clean?"

That was the Ruvie he knew.

Later, they sat side by side on the sofa reading their books. She started to talk without looking up from the page.

"Denzel, I'm going to stay here and wait out the end. If the whole world is doomed, it doesn't matter where I go. But you don't have to do what I do. If you want to go somewhere else, you can go ahead and take all the food in the house. You're still young, but you have the right to decide where you're going to be when the time comes."

He thought carefully about what Ruvie said. Then he asked the question he'd wanted to ask all day long. "Can I stay here?"

Ruvie looked up from her book and smiled at him.

After that, Ruvie was like her old self, mostly, except that she stopped doing the yard work. That became Denzel's job.

He could see construction starting at the Shinra Building. In no time at all, it seemed, an enormous cannon was towering over the city.

"Shinra's going to shoot that rock into bits!" he told Ruvie.

"Is that so? Well, I hope it works. But I wouldn't count on it. That company has never done a single thing right," Ruvie said dolefully.

In the end, the cannon fired just one volley at an unseen target before collapsing in a wreck. As if that weren't enough, the Shinra Building itself was attacked and destroyed. Denzel wondered what kind of monster could have done that. He couldn't even begin to imagine one big enough to take down a building that size, but he kept himself from asking Ruvie about it.

Up in the sky, Meteor still hung, unchanged. All hell may have broken loose elsewhere, but Denzel's days went quietly by.

Sometimes he missed his parents so badly that he sobbed aloud, but Ruvie would hold him tight, and then he felt better. She let him sleep in her bed, and he thought that if the end of the world came while they were asleep together, it wouldn't be so bad.

In the end, it wasn't Meteor that came to shatter Denzel's peace but a furious torrent of white light.

The Lifestream released by the planet may have effectively destroyed Meteor, but the dense life energy also inflicted untold destruction upon the world of mankind.

The chosen day. Denzel and Ruvie were in bed, trying to sleep despite the howling wind outside. Even for a gale, the noise was terrific. Then the entire house began to rattle.

This must be the end, thought Denzel. He hoped it would be over quickly. The tremors grew more violent, and the noise swelled to such a roar that a train could have been passing right outside the window.

Ruvie held him tight, and he squeezed his eyes shut, trying to brave it out, but five minutes proved to be his limit.

"Ruvie, I'm scared!"

Just as Ruvie got up to turn on the lamp, a blinding white light shone right through the drawn floral curtains. It was as if the house were being swallowed up by the sun.

"Get under the blankets and stay there!" Ruvie left the bedroom. The house shook even harder, and the vase of fake flowers on the dresser tumbled to the floor. Denzel jumped out of bed and went after her.

She was in the living room, staring at the window—the one he had broken and that she had covered with a tarp. The tarp was swelling like a balloon, looking as if it was about to burst open. Ruvie leaped forward to hold the tarp on with both hands.

"Denzel, get back to the bed!"

He was trembling uncontrollably, and his feet were glued to the floor. *I'm the one who broke the window. This is all my fault. Bad things are happening because of me!*

Ruvie dropped the tarp and darted toward him. Denzel clung to her even as she forced him back into the bedroom. At that same moment, the tarp blew away, and the dazzling light flooded the room.

She slammed the door shut just before she screamed.

"Ruvie!" Denzel yanked on the doorknob.

"Denzel, don't!"

"But—!" He pulled it open and found Ruvie standing there with her back turned to him, splayed against the doorframe to keep him in.

"CLOSE IT!"

Past her, he could see tendrils of light darting and twisting like snakes, striking the walls and bouncing off in every direction.

This thing's not in the monster encyclopedia, he thought. *I have to run and tell an adult. No—in this home, I have to do the fighting.*

"Ruvie!" he cried as the tendrils seemed to lunge at her. She let out a short groan. Slender fibers of light surged through the gaps between Ruvie and the doorframe, into the bedroom.

Ruvie crumpled to the floor, and in the same moment, Denzel was flung back by the radiance. He blacked out.

* *

"I don't know how long I was lying there. When I woke up, the whole house was a wreck. Ruvie was lying on the floor. I called her name, and she opened her eyes a little. She said she was glad I was okay, but she said it so quietly, I could barely hear her. Then she said she wanted to hold my hand.

So I held out my hand, and she took it, but her grip was so weak it was like her hand wasn't there or something. She said her son's hands had gotten too big for her to hold. That made me glad I was little. Then she asked me how it looked outside. I was scared to look, but I went out anyway. It was morning. And the whole area was just like our house. A wreck."

Denzel stared down at the table as he spoke. Reeve listened with his eyes closed.

*   *

Outside, Denzel turned to look back at their house and saw that none of the windows had any glass left in them. He turned in a circle, taking in the rest of the scene. The other houses were in no better condition—smashed windows, collapsed roofs, caved-in walls. *It would've happened anyway*, he realized. *It would still've gotten in and wrecked everything even if the window wasn't broken.*

As quickly as the thought came, he became mad at himself for thinking it. *Ruvie tried to protect me and got hurt badly because of it, and I'm trying to pretend it had nothing to do with me.*

He went back inside. Ruvie was sleeping. She looked so serene and peaceful, lying there. It made him uneasy, and he shook her shoulder.

"Ruvie."

But she showed no signs of waking.

"Ruvie!" He shook her again, harder.

A thread of black liquid trickled from the edge of her mouth. It looked like the mark of death to him, and he hastily wiped it off. But it was oozing out from beneath her hair, too. Denzel felt sick to his stomach. He staggered out of the house, seized with dread.

"Mom! Dad! Help!" he screamed at the top of his lungs. After that, he called out for everyone he knew, all the names he could think of.

No one came, and so there was nothing to do but sob.

"Hey, little guy. What're you crying about?" A big hand grabbed Denzel's head and turned his face up.

A great big man with a black mustache was standing over him. A small truck was parked beyond, with ten or so men and women sitting on the cargo bed.

"You shouldn't be out here. They told everyone to get to shelter down in the slums. Didn't you see it on TV?"

Denzel felt like the man would yell at him if he didn't give a good reply. "I haven't been watching TV," he managed through his sobs.

"Damn, what's wrong with you people? 'We didn't know! We thought we'd be okay!' It's the same story with the whole lot of you!"

The men and women in the truck looked at their feet sheepishly.

"So where're your folks?"

"Ruvie's in the house."

*   *

"The man's name was Gaskin. He helped me bury Ruvie in the backyard. The people in the truck pitched in, too. We buried her son's books and her sewing kit with her. Everyone thought it was weird that the soil in the backyard was so deep. Usually, you hit the Plate right away, they said."

"Perhaps she'd meant to raise vegetables. A lot of elderly folk from the country do that, you know."

"I… I think it was flowers," Denzel replied, looking down at the floral print handkerchief. "Her house was full of flower patterns, and she had lots of fake flowers, too. But I think she wanted real ones. She lived in Midgar because her son worked for Shinra, but she missed the countryside, and she wanted a nice place with soil where she could plant some flowers and… Sorry. This is boring, huh?"

But Reeve was hanging on to every word.

*   *

The truck carrying Denzel and the others eventually stopped at the departure terminal for slum-bound trains. Gaskin spoke up.

"The trains aren't running. No prospects of them starting up again, either. But if we're lucky, we should be able to walk down the tracks all the way to the surface."

"Is the city gonna collapse?" someone asked.

"Your guess is as good as mine. But either way, it's got to be safer down on the ground, right?" Then Gaskin turned to Denzel. "Watch your step, all right? Everyone's tired and at the end of their rope. You gotta look out for yourself."

Gaskin got back into his truck, made a U-turn, and drove away.

Masses of people were clustered in the station. That white light had taken its toll on all of Midgar, and those whose homes were ruined, and those who were afraid the city might fall, had come here to flee. However, now that they were actually here, more than a few of them were having second thoughts. It looked a dangerous proposition, clambering down those tracks.

No one was celebrating being saved from Meteor. Instead, they were angry about the botched and delayed evacuation order, and they were looking for someone to blame. *Good thing Dad's not here*, Denzel thought. He squirmed through the crowd to the platform, where he jumped down onto the tracks to join a growing stream of people.

He had no idea what would come next. But Denzel figured no one had given him any advice besides Gaskin, so he might as well do what the big man said.

Below his feet, between the crossties of the tracks suspended on their steel supports, he could see all the way down to the slums. If he slipped here, it would be a long fall to the ground. The tracks descended in a spiral winding around Midgar. It would be a sickeningly long journey, but Denzel put his head down, forgot about how far he had to go, and concentrated on making one careful step after another.

Suddenly, the crowd came to a halt in front of him. A dead end? Denzel pushed his way through the legs of the grown-ups to see what was causing the bottleneck.

There was a little boy, maybe three years old, perched on one of the crossties, kicking his feet in the empty air below him.

One of the adults spoke to him. "Where's your mommy?"

Out of the blue, the boy started wailing and yelling "MOMMY!" and stared down past his legs at the ground. He was on the verge of losing his balance when Denzel darted forward and grabbed his arm. Suddenly, there were gasps from the crowd.

"Hey, that kid's marked!" one said.

"Don't touch him! You'll catch it!"

What are they talking about? He didn't understand.

"Hey, get him out of the way!" someone shouted.

Seeing no other choice, Denzel dragged the boy to the side, where there was sturdier footing atop the iron sheets that connected the rails to the steel supports. He wondered why the grown-ups weren't helping, but then he saw the reason. The boy's back was wet with a sticky black fluid.

With the path cleared, people began to move again. The boy kept crying out in pain and screaming for his mother, but Denzel was thinking about the grown-ups' warning: "*You'll catch it!*"

He began to get angry at the boy, for being in the way and for crying and for maybe making him sick. But then he thought of Ruvie and how he recoiled in disgust at the black liquid, how he'd gotten scared and fled from someone who had been so kind to him. He felt terribly guilty.

So he decided to be nice to the boy to make up for it, and maybe make Ruvie forgive him. He crouched down next to the kid.

"Where does it hurt?"

"Behind…"

"Your back hurts?"

"Uh-huh."

Cautiously, Denzel put his hand to the boy's back.

When my tummy hurt, Mom would always rub it, and it would stop hurting. It was the same with bumps and bruises. Although maybe it only works when moms do it.

Trying to ignore the black gooey liquid, he rubbed the boy's back. He could feel him relax, and then the whimpering stopped, and the boy fell asleep.

Denzel sat there for ages. Maybe three hours, maybe more. He kept comforting the kid, taking breaks when his arm got tired. People on the descent would avert their eyes, pretending they didn't see them.

"I think he's dead, kiddo."

Denzel looked up. A haggard woman was standing over him. She was carrying a baby in a sling and holding hands with a girl around Denzel's age.

"He's wearing a girl's shirt," said the daughter. "He's *weird*. C'mon, Mom, can we go?"

Without a word, the mother removed the girl's blue coat and offered it to Denzel. "Here, use this."

The girl still had three layers on, and she looked relieved to be free of one of them. She wiped her sweaty face. "You can have it. It's my sister's anyway, and it's too big for me."

Denzel didn't see an older sister.

He glanced at the boy curled up beside him. He was too still, and his chest was motionless.

Suddenly, Denzel felt enormously tired.

The girl took the coat from her mother's hands and draped it over the boy, hiding his body from view.

"He's with my sister now."

"Thank you." It was almost more than Denzel could manage, just to get out that one phrase.

The woman was already walking away, and the girl scampered to catch up. She slid her hand into her mother's. Both hands were marked with black stains.

Denzel stared at the chocobo picture on the girl's backpack. *That black slimy stuff comes out of people's bodies, they cry because it hurts so much, and then they die. If the sickness is catching, maybe we're all going to die.*

*　　　*

"Back then, no one knew anything about the stigma. Everyone the Lifestream touched started oozing that dark slime, and then died. People said you could get infected by touching it. No one had figured out that it was actually the remnants of Jenova corrupting the Lifestream. Not that it would have made a difference, knowing."

"Especially for a kid."

"Right."

"I kept thinking on the train tracks that I wished I could grow up faster. Then maybe things would make more sense, at least a little bit."

*　　　*

Denzel at last reached the groundside station, where he gaped at the tide of refugees that trudged down from the Plate and on into the slums. He knew he should keep walking, too, but he wanted to linger in the hope of maybe spotting a familiar face in the crowd. But it wasn't long before a gnawing hunger overcame all other considerations, and he began wandering around the station in search of something to eat.

He came across a big pile of bags and, beyond that, a cluster of men who appeared to be digging a big hole. The smell of rot hung in the air. Another man came up carrying a young woman slung over his shoulder and gently lowered her into the ground. The men were digging a mass grave.

Denzel backed away from the scene and almost fell over the pile of bags and possessions. Looking down at his feet, he saw a backpack decorated with a picture of a chocobo.

Spurred by a sudden impulse, he grabbed the backpack and looked inside. It was full of cookies and candy. He thought of the girl it belonged to. But she was dead…

"Eat while you can."

It was Gaskin. Denzel realized he was the person he'd been vaguely hoping to find.

"Worried you'll catch the sickness? No one knows if it's actually contagious. It might be, or then again, it might not. But one thing's for sure: You've got to eat. Even if you're going to die anyway, might as well do it on a full stomach," he said as he reached into the backpack and helped himself to a cookie. "Not bad. Best chow down. No point letting 'em go to waste."

Denzel ate one, too. The buttery sweetness was comforting. Still looking down into the backpack, he said, "Thank you."

Gaskin ruffled his hair.

He's not like Dad at all, but he ruffles my hair the same way.

They ended up staying right there in the area around the station. His first job was finding food in the abandoned bags and belongings. He banded together with other children like him, orphans with nowhere to go but the streets. Gaskin made friends, too. *A bunch of idiots who aren't happy unless they're using their muscles to get stuff done,* he said. Some of them were the same men who had been part of the makeshift burial crew at the station.

During this time, Denzel occasionally caught himself smiling. It almost felt as if he'd gone back to being his old self. But after a few more weeks, the flow of refugees from upper Midgar thinned, and there were no more bodies to bury and no more abandoned baggage to search. Gaskin and his crew's role there was coming to an end. Denzel started to get scared again, wondering what would happen next.

One day, a man came by, searching the rubble for something. Eventually, he approached Denzel and his friends. "Listen, kids. I need metal pipes. Lots of 'em. Think you can find any?"

Denzel and his pals went hunting amid the wreckage and ruin of Sector Seven, and they came back with a fine haul. The man thanked them and left.

After that, the man kept coming back, always looking for more parts or materials. Sometimes, he'd bring along friends who were also searching for stuff. A new town was going up to the east of Midgar, and they needed materials for its construction. The kids brought whatever they could carry, and the people paid for their finds with food.

The Sector Seven Scavengers, they called themselves. Jobs were plentiful, and they felt proud to be working and living like adults. Plus, it was fun rummaging through the rubble looking for valuable prizes. Like treasure hunting. Sure, in the evenings sometimes, one or the other of them might cry for their parents, but they cheered one another up, like friends do, and they started to talk about how they'd be together forever.

However, destiny had not tied them together as tightly as they'd thought.

One morning, Gaskin assembled his friends—that is, the men in his crew and the kids of the Scavengers—and said it was time they moved to the new town so they could help with the construction efforts there. Just when they were starting to reach an agreement—let's do what Gaskin says—one of the kids asked a question. "Gaskin, are you sick?"

The girl had noticed him rubbing his chest as he spoke.

"Kind of." Gaskin unbuttoned his jacket. Underneath, his shirt was soaked black.

*   *

"A month after that, Gaskin was dead. Everyone came together and buried him in a nice spot. It's funny, but it seems like the good people always die first."

Reeve nodded solemnly.

Denzel took a sip of coffee. He hated coffee—it was so bitter—but he wanted to hurry up and learn to like it, like grown-ups did.

*   *

The men moved on, but about twenty of the kids stayed behind and continued on as the Sector Seven Scavengers.

They heard rumors about how the new town of Edge was growing by leaps and bounds, and they knew there were orphanages there. But they knew they were helping with the building efforts right where they were, and they liked getting by on their own wits. They saw no reason to walk away from what they had, and besides, they were too proud to go begging for protection as helpless orphans.

Progress, however, marches on, and their way of life was about to come to an end. Childish pride couldn't slow the development of Edge or stop heavy machines being used in the construction. In the time it took Denzel and the crew to haul a single iron girder to a customer, one of the big cranes could lift up a whole house and carry it off. Their numbers steadily dwindled as the children left, one or two at a time, until Denzel looked around one night and saw that only six remained of the original crew. And even with these few mouths to feed, they were hungry.

Then the last girl announced she was leaving for Edge.

*   *

Denzel chuckled.

"What's so funny?" asked Reeve.

"I hated that girl. The boys said having a girl along slowed them down, but whenever we split into groups, they all wanted to go with her. When there were a lot of us, it didn't matter so much. But toward the end, it was a real pain."

Reeve chuckled, too.

"But I realize something now. My being ticked off was a good thing. It meant I'd gotten to the point where I could sweat the small stuff. Like in normal life."

"Maybe you should thank her, next time you see her."

"Can't do that. She's dead now."

*   *

One morning, he woke up to find that the only Scavengers left were him and his pal Rix.

"All we can handle now are screws and light bulbs," Denzel said, laughing.

Rix grinned in reply. "Sure. But we'll corner the market and make a killing."

"I'll go find us breakfast. And maybe some work, too."

"Okay, hold up." Rix went over to where they stashed their cash box and opened the lid.

"Shit! Denzel, we've been crossed!"

They'd been left with nothing, not even enough for a chunk of bread.

The two sat for a while in silence. Rix was the first to open his mouth.

"Guess we've gotta go to Edge now. Find one of those charities that gives out food for free."

"You're giving up?"

"If you wanna call it that. I call it not starvin' to death."

Out of nowhere, Denzel recalled something his father had said.

"We could catch some rats."

"Rats?"

"Yeah. People in the slums used to do it all the time, right? 'Cause chicken was too expensive. I bet they taste okay, once you cook 'em."

"You serious?"

"Yeah. I'm gonna eat a rat. Like a real slum kid!"

Rix stood up slowly and brushed the dust from his clothes.

Denzel got to his feet, too, already looking around. "We need a stick."

"You're on your own, bud. This 'slum kid' is moving on. Been an eye-opener, though, findin' out what you topsiders thought of us down here."

Denzel realized his error and tried to smooth things over. "Look, sorry. I didn't mean it like that."

"Seemed clear enough to me. You think folk like my family and me ate rats like we were damn animals."

"No, that's not it!"

"Well, you don't know nothin' about anythin', dumbass. You're just another stuck-up brat from the Plate."

"Rix—"

"Here's somethin' else you don't know. Thanks to all the sewage you topsiders flushed down here, the rats are full of really, really bad germs. We wouldn'ta dreamed of eatin' them."

With that, Rix left.

*   *

Denzel sighed. "I didn't try to follow him. I figured he wouldn't forgive me."

"Why not?"

"Because he was right. I still didn't think I belonged down there. I stuck to the neighborhood around my station and the rubble in Sector Seven. I never thought of going anywhere else in any of the slums. And I didn't go to Edge, because I thought that would be just more of the same. All poor and dirty."

"What happened to Rix?"

"He's alive. Doing okay. But we don't talk."

"Well. As long as he's around, you still have a chance to patch things up with him."

*   *

Denzel found a stick, sharpened it into a mean point, and went looking for rats. He really did plan to eat one. *Dad, people in the slums don't eat rats. But I will. I don't have money or work. I'm a Sector Seven topsider, but it's just a pile of rocks and broken metal now. I don't belong here. I can't go on living here.*

Loneliness slowly stole Denzel's will to live. It was like after the fall of Sector Seven, but now no one was left to help him. His parents, Arkham, Ruvie, Gaskin, the Scavengers—they were all gone, and no more good things would ever come for him.

He felt like he'd never laugh again. *There's no point to a life without laughter. Doesn't matter now. The rats will help me. Them and their really, really bad germs.*

*   *

"Whoa, whoa—seriously?!" cried Johnny, who apparently had been eavesdropping.

"I'm just saying what I thought at the time. I know I was wrong. I'm still here, after all."

"Well, yeah. Sure."

"Because someone did come along," Reeve added.

"Uh-huh. Just when things were looking the worst."

*   *

There wasn't a rat to be found. He kept searching, though, aimlessly and listlessly, until he eventually reached the slums under Sector Five. He found a church there that was starting to fall apart. A motorcycle was parked in front of it. It was like no other bike he'd ever seen before. But what really caught his eye was the cell phone hanging from the handlebars. A smile came to his face. *I'll just borrow it for a second. It'd be funny if the call went through.* He took the phone and dialed the number for his house, imagining a phone ringing in the rubble of Sector Seven.

"All Sector Seven numbers are out of service."

He had asked around for information about his parents when he was working with the Scavengers, but he never found out anything. He figured they had been buried under rubble somewhere. It wasn't like he thought they were still alive.

"All Sector Seven numbers are out of service."

With the phone to his ear, Denzel looked up at the underside of Sector Five. Somewhere up there, he realized, Ruvie was asleep forever. He was standing beneath her grave. No wonder it felt so lonely here.

"All Sector Seven numbers are out of service."

He hung up. He thought about smashing the phone against the ground, then decided against it. *Just one more, let me try one more.* He was going to call Ruvie's house, but he couldn't remember her number. Actually, he had never known it in the first place.

It occurred to him to scroll through the incoming-call history. He decided to call the number at the top. This time it rang, and the person at the other end quickly picked up.

"Cloud, what a surprise. You never call. Is something wrong?"

Denzel silently listened to the woman.

"Cloud?" she asked warily.

"...No."

"Who is this? What are you doing with Cloud's phone?"

"I don't know."

"Who are you?"

"I don't know. I don't know what to do." His voice trembled.

"...Are you crying?"

He thought he felt tears. As he closed his eyes to wipe them away, pain shot through his forehead. It caused him to seize up and drop the phone. He hunched over double, holding his head. He felt something sticky on his hands.

I don't really want to die!

He tried to scream, but the pain wouldn't let him. So he prayed silently, as hard as he could. *Don't let it be the dark stuff. Don't let it be the dark stuff.*

Bracing himself against the throbbing pain, he opened his eyes. The palms of his hands were inky black.

*　　　　　*

"I don't remember anything after that. When I woke up, I was in a real bed. Tifa and Marlene were looking at me. The rest...you know already, right?"

"More or less."

"I'd be dead ten times over if it weren't for all the people who helped me. My parents, Ruvie, Gaskin, the guys in the Scavengers. People who are still alive and people who aren't. Tifa and Cloud and Marlene. Even..."

Reeve nodded like he knew already.

"I want to help people like people have helped me. It's my turn to do the protecting."

Reeve was silent.

"Please. Let me join." Denzel leaned forward in determination.

"No way, man!" Johnny interjected.

"You stay out of it!" Denzel snapped.

"You're just a *kid*!"

"That doesn't matter!"

"Actually," said Reeve, "the WRO no longer enlists minors."

"Aha! See?"

"Why didn't you just tell me that in the first place?" said Denzel sullenly.

"Because it's a brand-new policy. In fact, I decided it just now, while I was listening to your story. There are some things only kids can do. And I think you should be doing them."

"Like what?"

"Like helping grown-ups be strong when we need to be."

Denzel waited for him to say more, but Reeve stood up to indicate the talk was over.

"Oh, one other thing…," Reeve began.

Denzel stared at him expectantly.

"Thank you for taking care of my mother."

Reeve took a folded handkerchief from his own pocket and flicked it open. The fabric was covered in a familiar pattern of tiny pink flowers.

After Reeve left, Johnny began clearing the table. Denzel stared at his own handkerchief, laid out in front of him.

"You know, kiddo," Johnny said, "you can fight whenever and wherever you want, if that's what you're itchin' to do. What's so special about the WRO that you want to sign up?"

"Cloud."

"What about him?"

"He was in the military once. I figure that's why he's so strong. I want to be strong like him."

"Thing is, kid, times are changin'."

"Like how?"

"Well, lessee. Some guys can swing a mean sword and chase off monsters, while some guys're better at lookin' after folk and takin' away their pain. I'm thinkin' that in times like these, the ladies'll choose the latter over the former."

"I'm not doing it to try to get girls. Sheesh," Denzel said stiffly. But he was thinking of the people who'd ruffled his hair, the people who'd held his hand, the people who had made him feel liked when the world seemed to be falling apart. Whether they were men or women, grown-ups or kids…weren't those people the strongest of all?

He could feel the Lifestream incessantly trying to erode his spirit—his experiences, thoughts, emotions, and memories. If he gave himself over to the pull of the current, everything he was would be subsumed, his existence dissolved into the great spirit energy that circled through the planet. He would not let that happen. The planet was there to be ruled. To give it his own energy was to concede defeat.

He felt a surge in the Lifestream, a great upheaval—a sign, he knew, of another defeat. When the Lifestream burst out aboveground, it meant Cloud's victory was more secure than ever. Cloud had twice sent him into the Lifestream, and he would not allow it to happen again.

If he could only cling to the core of his consciousness, he could keep himself apart from the abyss and stay free of the planet and its insatiable appetite.

He had made his decision. Cloud would become the nucleus. He yearned to tell Cloud this.

I have not forgotten you. You are still in my mind. You do not know this yet, but soon, you will.

FINAL FANTASY.VII

EPISODE: TIFA

ON THE WAY TO A SMILE

Tifa was cleaning up after having seen off the last of Seventh Heaven's customers for the day. A short while ago, she would have done the work without care, but now in the dim gloom of the bar's kitchen, the water felt icy cold and the grime stuck stubbornly to the plates and pots. She tried turning on all the lights to lift her mood, but the unstable electric supply wasn't up to the task, and soon the lights dimmed again, bringing her mood even lower.

Do I really have to be all alone in this place?

Eventually, she couldn't stand it any longer and called her daughter's name. "Marlene!"

Before long, she heard cautious steps from the kids' room back behind the shop, and then Marlene poked her head out. "Shh," she hissed, finger to her lips, scowling in a childish rebuke.

"Sorry," Tifa whispered, though she immediately felt better despite the scolding.

"Denzel *finally* fell asleep."

"Was he hurting?"

"Uh-huh."

"You could've come to get me."

"He said not to."

"Oh." How pathetic was she, that a young boy was worried more about burdening her than his own illness?

"Did you need something?" said Marlene.

"Oh, um… I just…" Tifa hid her feelings as best she could, grasping for a neutral, lighthearted answer. Marlene's eyes shifted to the empty bar, and then back to Tifa.

"You're lonesome, aren't you?" Marlene sounded very grown-up when she said things like that.

"A little."

"I'm not going anywhere."

"I know. Thank you, Marlene. Now go to bed, okay?"

"That's what I was *trying* to do!"

"Sorry." Tifa left the dishes half-unwashed and followed her.

Marlene's parents had died a while ago, and her father's best friend, Barret, had taken her in. So Tifa had known her since she met Barret—nearly half the little girl's life. And since Barret had made up his mind to go off somewhere, "to settle some things," as he put it, it naturally fell to Tifa to look after her.

Denzel was sleeping in one of the two beds lined up side by side in the kids' room, his breathing soft and even. It was heart-wrenching to see the marks of geostigma on an eight-year-old boy. He wasn't getting worse, but he wasn't getting any better, either. The pain came and went, but when it was bad, it was…very bad.

With some wet gauze, Tifa dabbed at the dark bruising on the boy's forehead from which a dark liquid kept seeping. He winced a little but continued to sleep.

Marlene had been looking on, but now she crawled under the covers of her own bed.

"Tifa… You shouldn't be lonely. You have us."

"I know. I'm sorry." She meant it.

"It's okay. We have people we miss, too."

"Yeah."

"Hey, where do you think Cloud is now?"

Tifa shook her head. He was somewhere in Midgar, but she couldn't say where.

When Cloud didn't come back that time, she'd tortured herself with worst-case scenarios, like him crashing his bike or being ambushed by monsters. But then people would see him and report back. Tell her that he was still working, riding around the city and sometimes outside it. He hadn't been killed or hurt. He'd simply run away from home.

Usually, Tifa could pretend nothing was wrong, at least for the kids' sake, but it just wasn't in her anymore. Before long, they had figured it out, too.

"Why'd he go away?"

As if she knew. Maybe he had problems. With his life. With her. But then, she could remember the last smile Cloud had flashed at her—it had a kindness to it, as if to say, *Everything will be all right.* Or did she misread it? Did she ever know what he was thinking?

That day, the chosen day. Meteor, hurtling down from distant outer space, the Lifestream erupting from the planet to meet it above Midgar.

Just let it wash away everything, Tifa remembered thinking. *My past. Our past. And me, too.*

Even as she felt relief that the fighting was over at last, the first stirrings of an icy anxiety began to grip her chest.

Was she really supposed to just carry on regardless? Whenever someone else asked her the same question, she answered without hesitation: *Well, you have to go on living, no matter what happens.* And yet, when she posed it to herself, she wasn't so sure.

When the Shinra Electric Power Company developed mako energy and brought it to the masses, the whole world had prospered. But even as light spilled across the land, the shadows also deepened, and the anti-Shinra faction Avalanche had worked to expose those shadows to the public.

"They make mako energy by sucking the life out of the planet."

The exploitation of mako energy had already set the planet on a path to destruction. Avalanche tried to warn the people, to turn Shinra back from its suicidal course. And when no one listened, they resorted to increasingly extreme methods. Eventually, they blew up one of the Midgar reactors overlooking a heavily populated neighborhood.

But they miscalculated, and the bomb caused far greater destruction than they had anticipated, not only to the reactor but also to the surrounding areas. This finally brought the full wrath of Shinra down on the Avalanche cell.

What followed could only be called an atrocity. The company destroyed the entire strip of Midgar where Avalanche's hideout lay, inhabitants and all. Though they had not set the bomb themselves, Avalanche was—indirectly or otherwise—responsible for the loss of countless lives.

And Tifa had been a part of it.

She, too, had believed that Avalanche's lofty goals were worth the sacrifices. Along with the others, she'd buried the twinges of guilt beneath the narcissism of self-sacrifice, beneath the belief that she was putting her life on the line for the "greater good." That made everything fair game. With the dizzying pace of the events that followed, Tifa and the others never had the luxury to stop and think. And as their battle against Shinra gained its terrible momentum, another foe joined the fray. His name was Sephiroth.

That launched them on a new journey. With Tifa was Cloud, a boy she'd known back home; Barret, the other surviving member of Avalanche; and Aerith and Red XIII, who had joined them amid the chaos. The group set out from Midgar together and found more companions on the way—Cid, Cait Sith, Yuffie, Vincent—all with their own motivations to fight.

New friendships blossomed, but almost as if in payment, Aerith was taken from them.

But the quest continued. Once they felt the final battle drawing near, only then did Tifa find herself reflecting on all that had brought them to that pass and the decisions they had made without thought of victory or defeat.

For her, it had begun when she was only a girl. Trouble broke out at the mako reactor Shinra had built near Nibelheim, and the village—her home—was threatened. The company dispatched Sephiroth to deal with it, and he killed her father. She came to loathe Shinra and Sephiroth so much that it hurt. It was the easiest decision in the world to join Avalanche. Because of her grudge. Not to save the planet or humanity. The anti-Shinra and anti-mako slogans she shouted were just a righteous front for her own dark motives.

But even in the name of defending the planet, too many lives were taken. Never mind for the purpose of settling a personal vendetta.

The guilt, she knew, lay coiled within her, and she could only wonder how she was meant to go on living with that suffocating embrace around her heart. As she looked to what would soon be the ruins of Midgar, Tifa feared for her future.

But next to her, Cloud was watching the same scene and smiling serenely. That smile was nothing she'd ever seen during their travels. Cloud sensed her gaze.

"What?"

"Cloud, you're smiling."

"Am I?"

"Yup."

"This is where it starts. A new…" He paused, looking for the right words. "A new life," he finally said. "I'm going to keep on living. I think it'd be wrong to do anything else, after all that's happened."

"Yeah. I guess you're right."

"When I think of how many times I've told myself that, though, it makes me laugh."

"What do you mean?"

"'Cause I always screwed it up."

"That's not funny."

"But this time…I think it'll be okay." He thought for a bit before adding, "Because this time I have you."

"We've kind of always had each other, haven't we?"

"Yeah. But now I know what that means," Cloud replied, smiling again.

Together, they all went to visit Aerith, laid to rest in the deep, clear spring at the Forgotten City. The world she had given her life to save was okay now. That was what Tifa told her.

Then she heard someone asking, *What about you? Are you okay?* Was it Aerith's voice or her own? She couldn't tell. And she started to cry.

She hadn't gotten the chance to mourn when Sephiroth killed Aerith. Whatever sorrow she felt quickly turned into anger and hatred for their enemy. But now, coming to this place again, the unfiltered sorrow drove deep. Stricken, she realized: *I did this, too. The things I did with Avalanche made many people feel like I do now.* She sobbed harder. The tears wouldn't stop.

"I'm sorry. I'm so, so sorry."

She felt Cloud's hand on her shoulder. *He's holding me here, anchoring me so I don't get lost,* she thought. *I can cry as much as I want now. Then I'll be ready to lean on his shoulder. Because I sure don't know how to do this by myself.*

The journey had bound them all together, and yet, it was surprisingly easy to part ways. Vincent left with no more ceremony than a stranger on a train getting off at his stop.

"Hey, aren't we supposed to be friends?" Yuffie had protested.

It might have been Barret who made the point that, since they'd lived through it all, they could find one another anytime they wanted. Or maybe that was Cid?

Tifa and Cloud went to Barret's hometown of Corel. For Barret, everything had begun with the tragedy of Corel's mako reactor. He took one silent glance at the town and said, "Shouldn'ta come." Tifa remembered he had to live with his own guilt, too.

So they went to Nibelheim, the place that had once been home for Tifa and Cloud. But it didn't feel like a homecoming. It only brought back unwelcome memories that were all too vivid.

"We shouldn't stay here," Cloud had said. "I feel like we're getting dragged back into the past."

Tifa had been thinking the same thing.

*   *

Then they went to Kalm. Aerith's adoptive mother, Elmyra, was waiting there with Marlene, whom they'd left in her care. Both of them were staying with Elmyra's relatives, who owned a house there. Barret and Marlene were elated to see each other again.

As delicately as he could, Cloud broke the news to Elmyra about Aerith's fate. They couldn't be sure how she would take it, but the three of them apologized for not being able to save Aerith.

"I'm sure you did everything you could. You don't have to apologize to me," said Elmyra.

Tifa and the others had no answer to that. *Did we?* Did *we do everything we could?*

The usually sleepy town of Kalm was teeming with refugees from Midgar. Locals had opened their homes to serve as emergency shelters, and even the inn offered free rooms to the displaced city folk. But there were too many to be housed, and the unlucky ones without a room crowded the streets, all of them exhausted, many of them ill.

"They're sayin' it's contagious. I don't want Marlene coming down with that. Let's get outta here," Barret said with unmistakable fatherly concern.

"Yeah. Let's go," Cloud agreed.

"Okay. So we go. But where?"

"Back to our interrupted reality."

"Th' hell does that mean?" Barret huffed.

"Normal life."

"Great. Where're we gonna find that?"

"Don't know yet, but we'll find it." Cloud turned to Tifa. "Right?"

"Right!" Marlene piped up, full of energy.

Tifa nodded, too, but she was wondering, like Barret, where that normal life could possibly be.

The four of them arrived in Midgar, which was already bouncing back from the chaos of the Meteor near-strike and the aftermath. People were keeping busy building for the future—or at least, for the next day. The serpent of guilt in Tifa again tightened its grip. There were still so many people here, so many lives, and she had looked down from the sky thinking none of it mattered. Happy to see it all washed away.

Ashamed once more of her self-absorption, she confessed to Cloud and Barret what she'd been thinking on the airship. They understood, but they chided her for it all the same.

"It don't matter where we go or what we do," Barret had stated. *"None of us is gonna be outdistancin' our guilt anytime soon.*

"So we just gotta go on living," Barret said. *"Live out our days tryin' to atone. That's the only road we got."*

"It's not like you to get so weighed down," Cloud told her when they were alone.

"Well, it is now."

"No. You're stronger than that. And if you've forgotten how to be strong, I'll just have to remind you."

"You will, will you?"

"If I can," he managed, suddenly blushing.

At first, they had their hands full taking stock of the situation in Midgar. People lacked for every sort of necessity, and no one even knew where to start looking. Barret and Cloud and Tifa gathered info, then split up and spread the word, telling people where to find the things they needed, helping those who couldn't get them on their own. And at night they slept beneath the Plate, which everyone said would fall any minute.

One day, after Barret helped dismantle a house for materials, he brought home his payment in the form of a bottle of liquor, a kerosene heater, and several kinds of fruit.

"Get a load of this," he said with a smirk. With one hand, Barret deftly went to work preparing a cocktail. Tifa and Cloud gingerly sipped while Barret upended glass after glass, recounting memories of better days. The time he'd had too many and fallen down a well. How when he'd set out to propose to his dearly departed wife, he was so nervous that he drank until he had no idea which way was up, never mind what he was saying. The other two couldn't remember the last time they'd laughed so much.

The next day saw Barret looking serious and earnest.

"You know what someone's gotta do? Open a place where we can sell this stuff."

"Who? You and me?" Cloud replied, taken off guard.

"Not *us*, dumbass! You think either of us is cut out to deal with customers? Nah, it's gotta be Tifa."

"Me?" she said.

"You're the pro, aren'tcha?"

A bar called Seventh Heaven had served as Avalanche's base of operations, providing an income for its members and funding for its campaigns. Tifa had been the barkeep, manager, and whatever else she had to be to keep it running.

"Way I see it, Midgar folk fall into two groups," Barret continued. "The ass-draggers who can't accept what's happened to the town and the go-getters who are happy to take advantage of what they can. And hey, I understand how both sides feel. Everyone's got their problems, only difference bein' how they deal with it, right? But there's one thing that brings everyone together, right? Booze!"

"You think?"

"Look. Yesterday, we got hosed, and we were laughing. Like, for real. We were able to forget some stuff, huh? Just for a while, at least."

"It was a lot of fun."

"Right? People need that now! So, Tifa, whaddaya say?"

Tifa didn't have an immediate answer. She understood what Barret was getting at, but the idea of opening another bar felt like going back to the past—back to the Avalanche days.

"Give it a shot, Tifa. If it's too hard, you can always quit."

"Aw, damn, it ain't gonna be hard!" Barret argued. "If Tifa doesn't work, she'll just get to broodin', and 'fore you know it, she won't be able to do nothin' else."

He might be right.

So they began preparations. They found a location in the town that was springing up along the main road to the east of Midgar, and they started hauling construction materials from the city. Word got around, and soon they had a small army of volunteers, people they had helped with their modest intelligence network, who pitched in to build the roof and walls.

Barret boomed out orders like a parade-ground sergeant, while Cloud went around quietly issuing corrections. Tifa learned how to mix the drink and improve the recipe to make something that went down smoother. She also put together the bar's menu, using ingredients for which they could find reliable sources. Marlene became the official mascot, a morale boost for the folk laboring on the construction. New setbacks popped up every day, none of them easy to fix, but working through them gave all of them a sense of accomplishment.

Sometimes, when Tifa caught herself laughing, she would be stricken with guilt—what right did she have to be happy, after all the pain she'd caused? But then another crisis would need her attention, and as Barret predicted, she found herself with little time to brood.

When Cloud announced the place would soon be ready for its grand opening, Barret pointed out that it was high time they picked a name. They both had plenty of ideas, but Cloud's were uninspired, and Barret's sounded more like monsters to avoid than names for a bar. In the end, it was up to Tifa. Cloud and Barret promised not to complain about whatever she decided. But with the grand opening so close, there was more and more work to be done, and coming up with a name fell to the bottom of her list.

"Hey, um, did you pick a name yet?" Marlene asked shyly.

"Well, I'm still thinking," said Tifa. "Do you have any ideas?"

"I like 'Seventh Heaven.'"

It was the one name Tifa had been trying to avoid. "Why do you like that?"

"It was fun there! If we make another Seventh Heaven, we'll have fun again."

Of course. The grown-ups had been all wrapped up in their plots and lofty ideals, but for little Marlene, Seventh Heaven was just a happy home where Barret and Tifa and their friends hung out.

"Hmm. Seventh Heaven, huh?"

They couldn't erase the past. All they could do was come to terms with it and keep living. Tifa made up her mind.

Seventh Heaven was a hit from the day it opened. Anyone could mix a Corellian Gangbuster at home if they had a mind to, and the food wasn't much of a draw, truth be told. After all, there were only so many ingredients Tifa could reliably obtain. But even so, people were looking for just this sort of place—a place where they could spend time with friends and drink the evening away. A place where they could relish the present, or else forget it and dream about the future.

Customers without cash could barter for their tab. The menu featured plenty of juice and other drinks, so families could bring their kids, too. Only the drinks Marlene sampled and gave her seal of approval to made the cut. Indeed, she had become an indispensable presence in the bar. At night, before it got too late, she helped out as a waitress, and she was never shy about booting customers who'd had too much to drink.

Barret would nurse a bottle in the corner. Maybe he thought he was the bouncer, as unnecessary as that was. Cloud's job, meanwhile, was to obtain supplies for both cooking and distilling, but there were some hitches—turned out he didn't know a carrot from a gysahl green. At first, Tifa was amused that mighty Cloud's new life started with learning vegetable names—but then when she remembered why he was ignorant of such basic things, she thought better. *No, I shouldn't laugh.*

Cloud was not the best at the give-and-take of trade—which is to say, he was downright awful at it. Still, it was his job to acquire provisions, and the experience of negotiating with other people carried more value than the overblown prices he sometimes paid. Cloud was taking steps forward, and she was proud of him for it.

At the same time, though, she had to wonder if Cloud wasn't working himself too hard for her sake. A nervous thought struck her. *One day, the bar will be running nice and smooth—what if he decides to leave?*

She shook her head, as if to brush off the thought, and told herself firmly not to ask so much of the future when she had so much in the present.

It was actually Barret who first announced he was leaving. Satisfied with the bar's solid launch, he told them he had to leave Marlene behind and go somewhere.

"I gotta settle some things."

Tifa was upset, but Cloud only nodded quietly, as if Barret had already brought it up with him.

"Settle some things?" Tifa fumed. "We all have things to settle, you know."

"Yeah, but your job is to prove you can give and not just take. You can take care of that right here."

Then Barret left the shop, mumbling that he had to get ready.

"Did you know?" she demanded of Cloud.

"Yeah."

"You didn't try to stop him?"

"No. He said this is your place, where you belong, so..."

"I guess that's that, then."

Cloud... Is that what you think, too? Tifa wanted to ask.

The night before Barret was to depart, Marlene, who always slept in Tifa's bed, plopped down next to Barret instead. Tifa could hear them talking late into the night.

He left early in the morning. As he walked away, Marlene said:

"Send me letters, okay? And call!"

Barret made a small wave with his right arm, to which he'd attached a machine gun instead of the prosthesis he'd been using. His back was turned as if to say, *Fightin's the only way I know how to live.* What kind of life would he find? One that involved more than just fighting, Tifa prayed to herself. One where he learned how to give, too.

"Cloud and Tifa can be my parents for now! So don't worry—I'll take care of them!" Marlene said.

Tifa and Cloud exchanged a glance. Her parents?

Then Barret turned to bellow, "Yeah, you look out for 'em!" His voice broke a little. "Families gotta stick together!"

If she was to go on without being crushed under the weight of her guilt, she needed other people with her. Even if they bore the same wounds or if the same guilt sat heavy on their shoulders, comforting and supporting one another was the only way they could move forward.

Maybe we can call that a family. And in a family, people stick together. If we have each other, maybe we can weather this storm...and the ones to come.

"So we're family," she murmured.

"Yup!" Marlene chirped. "And you too, Cloud."

"Awesome," said Cloud, with conviction. He glanced at Tifa, and she gave him a tiny nod. There might still be trouble ahead. But she would stop worrying about what they were to each other, she decided.

It must have been several months after opening the bar. Tifa got a phone call from Cloud, who was out securing provisions.

He had a request. "Would it be okay to print up a lifetime voucher for free meals and drinks at Seventh Heaven? Just the one." Tifa agreed, never asking for a reason. She knew Cloud must have wanted something desperately if he was offering to trade something that odd.

Night fell, and Cloud came home on a bike unlike any she'd ever seen. After that, whenever he had a spare moment from the bar, he'd work on it. He brought home engineers he met who-knows-where and talked to them about souping it up. There seemed to be any number of them helping Cloud complete the bike. Marlene and her neighborhood friends would look on, transfixed. The sight reassured Tifa. *We're a family, and we're becoming a part of this world.*

Most days, Cloud went outside Midgar to find things, usually to Kalm. He often rented a scooter or truck, though he sometimes took a chocobo. But now, with his own bike to ride wherever and whenever, he could venture farther afield and surprise Tifa with hard-to-find produce.

One night, a call came in to Seventh Heaven for Cloud. He didn't talk for long before telling Tifa he was going out.

"Where?" asked Tifa.

"I'm not sure how to tell you this…"

Cloud explained that while procuring supplies, he was sometimes asked to deliver things back to Midgar. The phone call was from one of his usual sources for vegetables, who had an urgent job. A delivery, which had to arrive that very night.

Cloud had the look of a kid forced to confess a secret.

"Why are you looking so sheepish?"

"I just… Sorry I didn't tell you."

"Tell me what?"

"That I had this other job."

Tifa burst out laughing.

Then he explained that he felt bad for keeping it from her because there was money involved. He'd been taking the extra income and putting it into his bike. Paying for parts and upgrades.

Just like a little kid, Tifa thought. But she felt a pang, somehow, to learn that Cloud had found another world to live in, one she wasn't part of. At the same time, she was glad his horizons were broadening.

Maybe this was kind of what a mother felt like. Once she saw Cloud off, Tifa was alone with the new emotions growing inside her. She realized she was happy.

Tifa was getting better at dealing with her guilt. Not that she forgot any of it. Maybe one day she would be punished for her crimes, but until then, she would live looking to the future rather than the past. She would prove to herself that she could give and not just take.

Tifa suggested that Cloud turn the delivery service into a legitimate business. *You can take orders right from the bar. Marlene and I could cover the phone.*

Cloud was reluctant at first, but after sleeping on it, he agreed to the idea.

She wasn't sure why he dithered like that. She kept from worrying about it, though. Maybe he was just nervous about making his little business more legitimate.

Either way, that was the start of Strife Delivery Service. The company was based in Midgar, but from the beginning, they operated anywhere in the world. Well, wherever Cloud's bike could take him, at least. *Anywhere* was false advertising, Cloud had laughed.

Just like Seventh Heaven, the business boomed. In those days, getting something to somewhere else wasn't at all easy. There were still plenty of monsters around, and roads and railways everywhere were still broken and unrepaired after the upheaval of the Lifestream eruption. The work, which involved running from one corner of the world to another, was not something just anyone could do. There was a lot of demand for Cloud's services.

Cloud had a hard time dealing with people, and yet, he was helping bring people together through the things they exchanged. Tifa thought that was wonderful.

Their life as a "family" changed a lot when the delivery service took off. But not really for the better.

Cloud was hardly ever home, except in the morning and late at night. Naturally, the three of them had fewer chances to talk. Tifa closed the bar once a week, but that didn't necessarily mean Cloud could take the same day off. He almost never turned down a client. While she did wish he would take a day off with them now and then, she felt that was selfish and kept it to herself.

It was Marlene who noticed the changes in Cloud. "Sometimes he just looks up at the sky and doesn't listen to me," she complained to Tifa.

He had never really initiated conversations with Marlene in the first place, but he wouldn't ignore her when she talked to him, either. Tifa knew that Cloud tried to be considerate toward Marlene in his own way, the same as anyone who didn't quite know how to deal with kids.

"I bet he's just tired."

But despite her reassurances, it bothered Tifa. Marlene was an observant child, sensitive to the grown-ups' moods.

On their day off, Tifa and Marlene went to clean up the room that served as Cloud's office. One of the parcel slips lying around caught Tifa's eye.

Sender: Elmyra Gainsborough
Item: Bouquet
Destination: Forgotten City

She bundled it up with the other slips as if she hadn't noticed. But inwardly, she was in turmoil.

Flitting from place to place delivering packages, Cloud was brushing up against the past. She knew that his inability to protect Aerith still weighed heavily on him. He was trying to move past that and live for the future, but if he had to go back there, to the place where she had left them forever, wouldn't the sorrow and remorse come rushing back, tearing open those old wounds?

The next night, after Tifa closed up shop, Cloud was there at the bar drinking, which he rarely did. His cup was empty. She hesitated for a moment, then went up to him and poured him a refill. "Mind if I join you?" She had things she needed to say.

"I wanna drink alone," he said.

Tifa lost her temper at that, and she snapped at him.

"Then take a bottle to your room."

Barret would call from time to time. He never said what he was up to or how he was getting on. He only wanted to know how Marlene was doing, and then he'd ask to talk to her.

Maybe Marlene thought Tifa wasn't listening when she said in a small, lonely voice, "Cloud and Tifa aren't getting along."

Tifa made every effort to talk to Cloud. When Marlene was around, she tried harder. She would attempt to keep it light and avoid anything serious. Cloud seemed puzzled at the change in Tifa, but he responded well enough and tried to meet her halfway, as if he knew what she was trying to do. Marlene would join in, too, and Tifa started to think that maybe her efforts were paying off.

One morning, she passed on a funny story about one of the regulars.

"Yeah, that would drive me nuts" was Cloud's opinion.

"You guys are driving me nuts!" shouted Marlene.

Cloud and Tifa both stared at her.

"You told that same story before, and Cloud said the same thing!"

It wasn't going well. But they were together—because they were family. They lived in the same house, and they lived by working together. *Maybe we don't talk or laugh as much as we could. But we're still family*, she thought. Or at least, she tried to.

Later, she sat next to Cloud as he slept and asked the question she dared not ask when he was awake: "We're okay, aren't we?"

Of course, there was no answer, only the sound of his slow, even breathing. Was the fact that he slept here enough? Did that alone make them a family?

"Do you love me?"

Suddenly, his eyes opened, and he looked at her groggily.

"Hey, Cloud. Do you love Marlene?"

"Yes. I just don't know how to act around her sometimes."

"But we've been together for a long time now."

"Maybe I need more than just time."

"...And what about you and me?"

Cloud didn't answer.

"Sorry," said Tifa. "I don't know why I'm asking these things."

"Don't be sorry. It's...my problem." Cloud shut his eyes again.

"We could make it ours."

Tifa waited for him to say something, but he never answered.

Not long after that, Cloud brought Denzel home. The boy had borrowed Cloud's unattended cell phone and called Seventh Heaven.

Hearing another person's voice come from Cloud's phone filled Tifa with sudden dread. But after a few gut-wrenching minutes, Cloud came on the phone.

"What's going on, Cloud?" For some reason, he had trouble answering.

"That boy—is he okay?"

"Not really. He needs help."

"You could bring him here."

"It looks like…he has geostigma."

Tifa froze. That was the disease that had appeared in the wake of the Lifestream surge that stopped Meteor. No one knew where it came from or how to treat it. It affected people differently, killing some and leaving others seemingly as healthy as before. Some people claimed that it was contagious. From what Tifa had seen, she didn't think it was. But then, it was possible, right? What if this boy brought the disease into their home? What if Marlene caught it? And even if they were safe, it could be bad for business, if word got around they were housing someone with the disease.

But she had already offered their home, and she couldn't bring herself to rescind that because the boy was sick.

"They say it isn't contagious," said Cloud, as if reading her mind.

She realized that Cloud *wanted* to bring the boy home.

"Okay. Bring him."

"I'll come in the back way. Is there someone who can watch Marlene?"

"Sure."

Tifa was glad Cloud had anticipated her fears and was being so cautious about Marlene and the bar's business. She realized he hadn't expected her to say yes but wanted to bring him home anyway. She wondered why.

Later, after the boy regained some strength, Tifa heard his story. Once she did, she realized he was supposed to be here.

Denzel lost his parents in the destruction of Sector Seven. Sector Seven was destroyed as retaliation against Avalanche. I was a part of that, and so he's my responsibility. I have to raise this boy as best I can. Denzel only found Cloud so that he could come to me.

She explained to Cloud that she wanted Denzel to stay as part of their family. Cloud simply nodded quietly, and Marlene was thrilled.

At first, Denzel tried to insist he was here for only a short time. But as he pitched in at the bar and Cloud's office, he started to open up to them.

Business at the bar started to decline. Old regulars stopped coming. There were fewer new customers. The adults knew why, but of course they said nothing, and taking Tifa's and Cloud's cue, neither did Marlene.

After dark, when the bar was closed, Tifa looked up from the dishes in the kitchen to see Cloud, president of Strife Delivery Service, seated at the center table with his assistants, Marlene and Denzel. The stigma never left Denzel, but there were plenty of days when the pain and fever subsided—time he spent tagging along with Cloud.

Typically, Cloud was out most of the day for work. The hours after he got home were important to Denzel; they were time spent with his hero. And yes, to him, Cloud was a hero. Of course, given how he and Cloud met, how Cloud came to his rescue when the symptoms of geostigma appeared without warning. And all the while, Denzel had to struggle with the fear of death.

He wanted to ask Cloud everything; even if he had questions Tifa could have answered, he would wait until Cloud got home. Once, half-jokingly, she told him that she was the one who cooked the meals, so he owed it to her to open up more. Denzel put on a grown-up voice and informed her that he was the one who cleaned up the bar and the house, so they were even.

That was true enough. Denzel was a thorough cleaner. When she asked him if he learned that from his late mom, he said no. Days later, Cloud told Tifa all about the woman who taught Denzel to clean. *He told Cloud but not me.* It made her upset. *Why won't he talk to me, too?*

It bugged her so much, she even complained about it to one of the regulars. "Oh, that's just how boys are" was the answer she got. "Sounds like normal, healthy family stuff to me." She wasn't entirely convinced, but she liked those words. *Normal, healthy family. Wouldn't that be great if it were true?* Sometimes after closing, she'd look at the three sitting around the center table and see a young father and his two children. And when she came to join them, they would always welcome her with grins.

Cloud would have a map spread out to plan routes for the next day's work, while Denzel and Marlene sorted the orders. When Marlene got to a name she couldn't read, she would ask Denzel, and he would tell her, proud to be the smart older brother; but if he couldn't read it, either, he'd ask Cloud. Cloud's custom was to hand them a pen and tell them to write it out a few times, saying they needed to get the spelling right to learn it properly.

Then, as they matched the names on the order slips to the names on the map, Marlene and Denzel would beg Cloud to tell them what those places were like. Cloud would give the briefest of descriptions: lots of people, hardly any people, crawling with monsters, going in from the north is safer.

Tifa wondered if the children were satisfied with the short answers, but they seemed happy enough. She always wanted to tell them more, and when she did, Denzel would turn to Cloud and ask if the details she gave were true. That bugged her, too. But then again, didn't that just mean he felt comfortable with both of them? In real families, kids and parents always had favorites. *Normal, healthy family stuff. Right?*

She started to think that bringing Denzel into their circle had made it more complete. That it had bound them together into a real family. Cloud was cutting back on his workload and making more time for the kids in the evenings, and the silly little everyday conversations they used to have were starting to return.

"So did you work out that problem?" Tifa wondered.

"What problem?"

"Your problem."

"Oh." Cloud fell into silence.

"It's okay if you don't want to talk about it."

"No, I do. It's just…I don't know if I can explain it right," he said. "I haven't worked it out. I mean—there is no way to work it out. Once someone's gone, there's nothing anyone can do, right?"

Tifa nodded.

"But now, I've got another chance to save a life. And I'm thinking, maybe…it's possible. Even for me."

"Denzel?"

"Yeah."

"Do you remember the day you brought Denzel home?"

"Sure."

"It sounded to me like you'd made up your mind to bring him in whether I liked it or not."

"No, I—" Cloud looked like a child who knew a scolding was inevitable.

"Just tell me. I'll hear you out first before I decide whether I'm mad."

Cloud nodded.

"I…" He paused. Then, in a torrent: "I found Denzel on the ground outside Aerith's church, and I thought she must have led him to me."

"You were at the church."

"I didn't mean to keep it from you."

"But you did."

"I'm sorry."

"Why? I never told you not to. But next time, I'm going with you."

"Okay."

"But, Cloud, you're wrong."

He gave her an uncertain look.

"Aerith didn't lead Denzel to you."

"I know. It's just how it felt, is all."

"That's not what I mean," Tifa said softly. "She led Denzel to us. To our family."

Cloud held her gaze. Then he smiled.

Only a few days after that, he was gone. She thought she'd seen a promise of a future in that smile. *Did I imagine that promise?*

Tifa kissed the children's sleeping faces and went to Cloud's office. She brushed a thin layer of dust from a photo of them all together. Then she picked up the phone and dialed. It rang several times and then went to voice mail.

She was an Ancient. Thus, she was able to retain her own selfhood even within the flow of the Lifestream. When she wished it, she could dissolve that self and become part of the planet forever, but it was too soon for that. *Just a little longer*, she thought.

She could feel an aberration in the coursing Lifestream, an implacable will that refused to merge with the planet. She knew it was the man who had killed her. A man whose fine, handsome features had hidden the vicious spirit that now plotted and schemed within the Lifestream. She sensed he was trying to exert his power in the corporeal world. She wanted to stop him. But how?

It was too dangerous to come into contact with him. She stayed far away from his cruel consciousness. That made it harder to discern his intentions, but the one time she did stray dangerously close, she learned something important. His memories of Cloud formed the core of his will.

Cloud was her friend. More than a friend, for she had loved him. He was a symbol of everything she held dear. She would protect him.

FINAL FANTASY.VII

EPISODE: BARRET

ON THE WAY TO A SMILE

Months had passed since the chosen day. After helping Tifa and Cloud build a new home, Barret entrusted Marlene to them. She was the orphaned daughter of his best friend, Dyne, and knew only Barret as her father. But he had to leave her behind when he set out on a journey to settle the sins of his past.

Before departing, he gave some advice to Tifa, who shouldered the same guilt. *Don't just take. Prove you know how to give.* He thought doing that would lead her, at the very least, to some kind of redemption. But his own advice brought him no solace, and Barret remained unsure of what he was supposed to do. Being with Marlene gave him peace of mind. It was easy to stay with her, even if he felt guilty for putting off action just one more day. He knew he had to leave, even if he had no destination in mind. Put some space between him and his heart's crutch, bare himself to the wilds. Don't think about it; just do it.

For half a year, Barret wandered the world. Geostigma was spreading beyond the walls of Midgar, but apart from that, life had mostly returned to a semblance of normalcy. The only difference was that hardly anyone used mako, and all the reactors, every last one, had been shut down. This was exactly what Barret and his comrades had once sought with their anti-Shinra operations, and yet the victory had left him aimless. What place was there for a man with a gun attached to his arm in a world free of war and turmoil? How could he redeem himself when there were no more battles to be fought? These questions plagued him.

Sometimes, he tramped into deep forests in search of a fight, taking down the monsters he found. But after, the adrenaline rush would fade, and he would sink into self-loathing. *What am I doing out here, just venting stress?*

All he could do was roar in fear and frustration.

It happened when he was picking his way through a crowd in Junon. Barret felt something collide against the metal plates of his weaponized arm, and he lowered his gaze to see a small boy beginning to cry, blood running down his forehead.

When he moved to help, a woman who had to be the boy's mother dashed between them. "Please. He's just a child. He didn't mean to— Please, I'll give you anything you want—"

The mother's terror-filled eyes were riveted on the machine gun that served as Barret's right hand. *In peacetime, I'm just another monster*, Barret thought. The times were changing, and he knew he needed to change with them...just not how. If he didn't, though, he'd never be able to atone in this world of peace.

Barret paid a visit to Old Man Sakaki in Corel. The wiry old-timer with white hair cut military-short was a skilled technician, single-handedly responsible for maintaining all the mining equipment in the village. When the people of Corel abandoned the coal mines and set their hopes on the mako reactor, he'd left town without a word of farewell. But then later, when the Shinra Company turned its back on Corel, he returned and settled in a house some distance outside the village, where he set about playing the role of local eccentric.

It was Old Man Sakaki who had first come to Barret, pestering him with offers to build him a prosthetic hand. At first, Barret was irritated by the suggestion, even more so when the old-timer explained his motivation—he'd never made a prosthetic before and wanted a challenge.

What kinda reason is that? Barret thought. But then again, he was finding life with one hand difficult. Maybe the crazy old man could help?

"Fine. So long as I don't have to pay for it," he had said at last.

The first model was a simple hook. Barret was not impressed. He wanted to be able to *do* things, like dig trenches or hammer nails. So the old man made him a shovel attachment and a hammer attachment. It still wasn't enough.

Barret told him so, and Old Man Sakaki had words of his own for him.

"You're just out for revenge on Shinra. You won't be satisfied no matter what you put on that arm. Here, take this and get out. And don't come back."

The old-timer shoved a new piece at him, a sort of adapter to fit on the stump. It would let Barret attach any sort of tool he wanted. Even a weapon.

"Now you can outfit yourself however you like. But you'd best think long and hard about what you choose."

If that had been a warning, Barret never heeded it. For the next several years, the only things he attached to his arm mount were weapons. Anything that made him more powerful—and more deadly.

Despite how much time had passed since their last meeting, Barret gave Old Man Sakaki the barest of greetings before asking for a new prosthetic.

"Something softer," he said, "more like a hand. Something that'll let me fit in. Something that won't scare the wits out of regular folk."

Old Man Sakaki only stared at him dubiously, with one cocked eyebrow.

"I'm not just about fightin'. I don't want people 'fraid of me no more," Barret elaborated.

"So who are you trying to be?"

"I'm *saying*—," Barret started, only to realize he didn't have the answer. *How am I supposed to fit into a world where people are learning how to smile again?*

"Damn! Th' hell if I know!"

"I'll need a week. Good with you?"

"Yeah. So in the meantime, could I—?"

Barret was about to ask if he could stick around while he waited, but the old-timer cut him off. "If you've got nothing else to do, you could help out my nephew with his work. Dunno if he can pay you, but…"

"Money's one thing I don't need."

"All right. I'll talk to him."

The next morning, Barret climbed into a steam wagon driven by Old Man Sakaki's nephew. People had used coal-burning wagons like this for everything when he was a kid. It took four people working together to operate the vehicle—a driver at the wheel, an engineer spinning the valve controls, and two stokers to keep the fire burning and the tank steaming. Behind the hulking engine was a bed big enough for ten sturdy grown men. Half the space was piled high with coal. Barret stretched out in the space that was left.

He lay on his back, gazing up at the sky. *Man, this is slow goin'.* Not that anyone was to blame for it. These big steam wagons had never been built for speed. The crew sweated just with the effort to keep it ticking over. Men and machine alike were running at full capacity.

A middle-aged man, one of the stokers, climbed back for a break. "Sorry to intrude on your stewin', but I need a breather."

"Stewin'? I ain't stewin'."

"Son, there's more steam comin' off you than that there engine."

Barret sat up, glaring murder at him. "You got a problem with me?"

"See what I mean?"

They rode in silence for a bit until the stoker struck up conversation again.

"You fixin' to be our bodyguard for good?"

"I'm just here 'cause Old Man Sakaki asked me. Dunno what I'm doing after this."

"Yeah. Don't seem like your kind of gig."

"What, bein' a bodyguard? You won't find nobody better 'an me."

"That a fact?"

With that, the stoker fell silent again.

Barret waited. *What does this guy think I am?*

"Hey, don't stop now. You got somethin' to say, let's hear it." *Well, if he's got so many damn opinions about me, one of 'em's bound to have something to it.*

"You look like the sort of fella who goes lookin' for the monster den, rather'n just worryin' about the ones that come at you."

Well, he might be right about that.

"Even if you don't know where the den is," the stoker added with a grin.

"You're saying I'm a fool?"

"I'm sayin', livin' like that can't be easy. Maybe you oughta be proud, eh?"

Barret stared at the man for a few seconds, and then broke into a low chuckle. Puzzled, the stoker looked back.

"Can I ask you about somethin'?" Barret said.

"Depends what the something is."

"Look, I've done some bad stuff, and I wanna make up for it—that's why I'm out here on the road. But I can't figure out how. And I'm prob'ly just the kind of guy you say I am. So whaddaya think a guy like that's gotta do to atone?"

"Well, depends on what you've done."

"…A lot of people died because of me. More than I can count."

Barret recounted the time he blew up Mako Reactor One with his comrades in Avalanche. The damage far more terrible than they'd planned. The panic that gripped the city. The friends he'd lost and the civilians he'd never even known.

After Barret had fallen silent, the stoker said, "You gotta stand tall and live, that's all. Just keep on tryin' whatever you think it takes to make amends."

"Keep doin' what I'm doin', only better…"

"So what if you don't know where the monsters' den is at? Go root 'em out. And if you keep at it, one day, there won't be no more—aw, hell, there's one of 'em now!" The stoker pointed toward the rear at a small but sinister monster that was gaining on the wagon.

Without bothering to aim, Barret casually raised his right arm and fired. The sound of automatic gunfire rent the air, and bullets tore through the hapless creature.

"Damn. He sure chose the wrong wagon to chase," said the stoker.

Barret was about to downplay his accomplishment, but when he turned back to the stoker, he saw that the man's gaze was fixed on his right arm. It was the same look the woman in Junon had given him.

"You know, man, the monsters' den might be somewhere inside me." He said it half in jest, but the stoker didn't laugh.

The wagon took them to a smaller village that survived by growing potatoes in the surrounding fields. Half the coal in the bed was gone by now, and they filled the cleared space with gunnysacks of potatoes. As he helped move them, Barret wondered how much these potatoes would go for in the city. Not the price the villagers set, that's for sure. The wagon crew had to be paid, for starters, and who knew how many others got a cut along the way. The price of food in Midgar was becoming a problem. Too high, even in these messed-up times. But looking around him, at all the folk working hard to get the food to market, he realized there was nothing to be done. With the mako gone, most of the farming machinery sat silent and useless. Growing and transporting potatoes took a good deal more manpower now.

"Hey!" Barret exclaimed, struck by a thought.

Without machinery, people had to rely on the strength of their own arms. And there was no shortage of people. *Midgar's full of folk beggin' for work and strugglin' to feed themselves. Sure, they can still forage outside town, but dammit, they can't do that forever. They need to till the soil, sow crops, plant seedlings, raise livestock.*

Barret was pleased. He was onto something.

If everyone put their minds to it, at least someday they could live in a world where no one had to go hungry. When they needed machines, well, they still had coal for things like the steam wagon. People just had to go back to the age before mako. There might be lean times ahead. And yes, life would be simpler. Duller, maybe. But that was the only way to go. The times had to change.

Barret smiled to himself, pleased with how easily he'd come up with the whole idea. Then he started considering his place in it. *Okay, so what kinda stuff can I do?*

He could attach a hoe to his arm and dig furrows. And a man his size could do the work of two others—heck, five others. But come to think of it, this new future would need leaders, too. *Should that be me?* His mind kept running. He imagined himself directing the work, bellowing instructions, men jumping at his every word.

"Got it, Barret!"

Jessie dashing from the room, Wedge and Biggs right behind her.

A scene from his days as the leader of Avalanche flashed through his head, and in an instant, his bright vision of the future was overshadowed by remorse.

Barret roared in frustration.

Damn, there I go again, he thought, and he glanced around. But no one was looking at him. Everyone's attention was on Old Man Sakaki's nephew, who was standing in someone's front yard deep in discussion with a middle-aged villager. Barret moved closer to hear the conversation.

"Mister, I can take your daughter to Midgar. That's not a problem. But she looks real sick. I'm afraid we wouldn't make it in time."

"Please. I'm begging you…"

The local man was carrying his daughter on his back. She was a lovely girl, but her head nodded weakly, and black fluid dripped from her arm onto the ground. A bad case of geostigma. This was the kind of situation

Barret hated most: *Right now, there's a crisis in front of me, and I can't do a damn thing about it.*

He knew there was no real cure for the girl in Midgar, either. He should probably tell them. Wouldn't it be better to let her spend her last days at home, in comfort, with her family? And yet, if he told them what he knew, the man would be condemned to watching his daughter die without even a ray of hope. *Maybe best to keep my mouth shut,* he thought.

"Wouldn't goin' to Midgar just be a waste of time?" asked a voice. Barret looked beside him and saw the familiar face of the stoker, scowling.

"Prob'ly," replied Barret.

"Then I better tell 'em," said the stoker, and he started to walk toward the man and his daughter.

"Hold up."

Barret went after him, hoping to stop him before he could shatter the father's illusions. The stoker sighed and turned around, frustration in his eyes.

"You think we should just let her go to Midgar? Even if there ain't no point?"

"Yeah."

"Well, the problem is, all we got ourselves is a steam wagon. The bed gets hot. It's a hard ride. You know that. What do you do when she ends up dyin' 'cause of it?"

"Still, come on, man…"

"Don't worry—I'll be the one to tell 'em. Maybe it'll kill her pop's hope. But the girl should spend her last days at home."

Barret didn't know if he or the stoker had the right of it. His mind was whirling. He needed to think. Again, he wanted to cry out, but he held it in.

In the end, though, it didn't matter. The stoker came back without ever talking to the father. "Didn't need to say nothin' after all. Poor girl died while they were talkin'."

"What?!"

"Do you wanna know what her last words were?"

Hell no, Barret thought. But the man was already telling him.

"'Please take me to Midgar,' she said." The stoker clenched his fists. "I couldn't have been more wrong."

"Grrr! No, you weren't! Nobody was, dammit!"

With no target for the rage surging up inside, he pointed his arm at the sky and fired, shattering the quiet of the sorrowful village.

Barret stayed behind to help lay the dead girl to rest. When it was done, the father lingered, staring with hollow eyes at his daughter's grave.

"Is there anything else I can do for you?" Barret asked as gently as he could.

"If only we had an airship," the man murmured. "I served on the *Guernica*. Maybe if she were still flying, my little girl would be alive. It's just a short hop to Midgar by air."

"Well, mister…" *I've got to say it now*, Barret thought. "I know how you must be feelin'. But there ain't no cure for the stigma in Midgar, either."

If only this. If only that. When you started brooding over the chasms between what was and what could be—what should be—you lost sight of the world in front of you. Barret had learned that lesson himself, the hard way. And lamenting things you could never hope to control, the way this father was doing now, was even worse. But before Barret could turn those thoughts into advice, the man started to speak.

"It doesn't have to be Midgar. It could be anywhere. If we found out that somewhere in the world there's a cure for geostigma, an airship could take people there. We'd…be ready."

"Ready?"

"To help the next victim. My daughter won't be the last."

He had only just lost his own child, and yet, he was already looking at what lay ahead.

The idealized pastoral future Barret had imagined while he was loading the wagon had vanished. *Why can't we run just a few of the airships and the other useful machinery? Hell, in Midgar, they're still using construction vehicles. Why not an airship, then? So long as we don't waste the mako. Times have changed, and I'm gonna do the same.*

*　　　*

A barren scrubland, many miles across, stretched out east of Rocket Town. Somewhere in that expanse stood a small refinery and an oil well 160 feet deep—both had been built many years ago. On this day, several dozen people were staring up at the derrick, among them Shera in her white lab coat.

A man in overalls stood next to her. "We're down seventy percent from last month. Not doing so hot. How about your end?"

"It's going well. We're nowhere near the efficiency of mako, but with our latest refining techniques, we're hitting higher numbers than ever," Shera replied.

"I knew you could pull it off. Doesn't mean a thing, though, if the well runs dry." The man looked down at the ground.

Shera looked down, too, thinking of the drill that plunged deep under their feet, blindly seeking out more precious oil.

"Just give us a little more…," she whispered, her hands pressed together in prayer. There was a black smear on the back of her left hand, but it was not oil.

It was geostigma.

*　　　　*

Rocket Town had once served as a base for Shinra's space program. The company engineers eventually settled here, forming a bustling rocket-science community, even though their expertise was no longer needed.

The first thing Barret saw as he strode into town was a roving cluster of laughing children, one of them the same age as Marlene. He broke into a smile. "Whatcha up to?" he called to them. The children all stared at him. "How 'bout you let an old guy join in?"

They ran away. Barret looked down at his right arm, clicking his tongue in frustration.

"Guess I gotta wait till I get my new hand."

"You're pretty scary even without the gun," someone remarked from behind him.

"Hey, you're…" Barret couldn't think of where he'd met the guy.

"I was one of the crew on the *Highwind*, but it's okay. I wouldn't expect you to remember me."

That was the airship that had flown them around the world on their quest to save the planet. "Oh, I gotcha. Tough times, they were. Thanks for helpin' out."

"We were happy to play a part."

Barret wasted no time asking the man to take him to Cid. As they set off, they heard a dull metallic pounding.

"Break's nearly over. We'd best hurry."

"What're you workin' on?"

"We're Cid's people. Take a wild guess."

"An airship?"

"Give the man a prize!"

Beyond the rows of houses, in a wide-open field, Barret could see an enormous airship under construction. *Just like the old* Highwind*!*

"Damn. That's a helluva sight!"

Twenty or so local workers scrambled around on crude scaffolding, which looked to score a solid F on a safety inspector's report, if they still had them. They hammered industriously at metal sheets that formed the hull, the high, ringing din echoing over the town. The airship looked all but finished.

"Hey, she's done!"

"Nah, it just looks that way. See?" The man pointed at the empty engine bay. "Mako's not an option anymore, so the engine's taking a while."

Suddenly, they heard an explosion, and Barret's combat instincts sent him diving into the dirt.

"Cap'n's over there." The former crewman laughed, pointing to a garage behind the airship.

Inside the garage, a single engine that looked like it would fit the airship sat upon a massive workbench. Several people, all of them wearing goggles, were peering at it from a safe distance. There was another explosion, but this time, Barret just flinched. One of the men threw down his goggles and stalked toward the engine.

"Sonuva—!" Cid started poking angrily at the faulty equipment with a wrench. "Goddamn piece'a shit! I'm gonna flatten you into last week's scrap!"

Barret grinned. It had been a long time since he'd heard cussing in that distinctive drawl. *This guy never changes.* Still spouting a stream of invective, Cid came over to Barret.

"You keep talkin' like that, an' God's gonna take issue," Barret said.

"God? You haul his ass down here," snapped Cid, not missing a beat. "See if *he* can get this blasted engine goin'!"

The two filled each other in on recent events. "I left Marlene with Tifa. Since she's taken to her and all."

"Gotta do what you gotta do, right? So Cloud's with Tifa, too?"

"Yeah. Tifa up and opened a place, like she used to have. Cloud was lending a hand, but now he's gone and gotten his own business. Delivery or somethin'."

"Cloud? Runnin' a *business*?"

"I think it's Tifa's doin'. She keeps him focused."

"Bet she does. When it gets down to it, it's the women who wear the pants."

"How's Shera?"

"Same as ever." Cid shrugged and abandoned the subject. "So what d'ya want? I've got my hands full here."

"Building an airship, huh?"

"Tryin' at least."

"Maybe I could help out."

"How? You don't know shit about airships."

Usually, Barret would lose his cool at an insult like that. But this time he let it slide, and instead he told Cid about what he'd been thinking.

"If we had airships, man, just think of all the lives we could save. Like people with geostigma. If someone ever finds a cure, you could get it to everyone fast. Or fly in experts who know how to treat it, to anywhere in the world. Or haul food, instead of cartin' it for days on a steam wagon. All the stuff people need to live, y'know?"

"You make it sound damn easy there." Cid leaned close, right in his face. "But we're talkin' airships. You know how much energy it takes to push these things around?"

"Not a damn clue. But listen..."

Barret recounted what he'd been mulling over on the road. That they just had to keep from getting greedy with the mako. Sure, it drained the planet's life. Nothing they could do about that. But it wasn't that much, right? The planet wouldn't mind them taking what they needed to keep folk alive.

"Damn. Am I hearin' this from the same knucklehead who used to run Avalanche?"

Barret had no answer for that. As for coming to terms with his past, he'd thought he'd found an answer. But hearing Cid pick it apart, he realized he didn't have the arguments to defend it. The familiar anger and frustration began to build in his chest. He raised his arm to fire off a volley, then remembered they were indoors. Instead, he roared.

Everyone in the room turned to stare.

"Sorry. Don't mind me." With a fierce effort, he forced his face into a grin meant to convey, *Just messin' with ya*. He stared hard at the floor, still groping for words, but all that came to mind were images of bygone days. Biggs, Wedge, Jessie. Earnest, trusting faces. *Say something. It's my fault. C'mon, blame me.*

He shook his head, trying to get his dead friends out of his mind, and looked up. Cid seemed out of focus.

"What the hell's wrong with you?" asked Cid.

"I dunno what to do, Cid. My past's like a minefield of mistakes. But I had to have done some good stuff, right? But which stuff? What was right? What was wrong? Which me am I supposed to be from now on? I wanna change, you know. But maybe I'm not allowed. Maybe I'm supposed to spend the rest of my life with a gun for a hand, scarin' kids everywhere I go. But how do I atone for anything that way? I don't know anymore. Help me. Tell me what I'm supposed to do!"

And in the end, Barret did open fire, tearing ragged holes in the ceiling. Cid looked at the damage.

"You can patch that up, for starters."

It was hard work, fixing the ceiling, and the sweat soaked Barret's shirt. When he saw Cid come sauntering over, Barret ignored him and kept working. He was still embarrassed over his outburst.

"You calm down yet?" Cid sat down, keeping his distance.

"...Sorry."

Cid shook his head, as if to say, *Don't worry about it*. "I thought of a way for you to help."

Barret stopped and looked at him.

"First off, about the mako. I think you're right. We could take just a little from the planet. Only what we needed, mind, and not a drop more. We were kinda thinking along the same lines out here. Truth is, airships are a real boon. Especially when we're talking about rebuilding the world. If one day they tell me, 'Hell, we don't need 'em anymore,' well, fine. I'll park her somewhere with a nice view and settle in. But until then..."

Cid went on to explain the current energy situation. Not a single mako reactor in the world was operating now. But it wasn't just because everyone suddenly felt bad for squandering all that energy. There was a practical issue, too. Without Shinra's organizational expertise, it was near impossible to keep the reactors running.

"But the real reason why the reactors are shut down is everybody now knows that mako energy sucked out the Lifestream and consumed it," said Cid. "And on that day, they all experienced firsthand how terrible the Lifestream could be. They're scared. Scared of pissin' off the planet."

Barret remembered Meteor drawing near in Midgar's sky, so close to obliterating the planet, and the Lifestream surging with overwhelming power to save them all. *That unstoppable power. Humans will never come up with anything like it.*

"Ain't nobody wants to make any more of that stuff now," said Cid.

"So that's it? No more mako production?"

"Ayup. Once the leftover reserves are used up, that'll be it."

"But c'mon, man. What's wrong with spinnin' up just one of them reactors now and then? How bad could it be?" *Biggs, Wedge, Jessie... Forgive me.*

"Even if we wanted to, the current reactors are no good where they are. The Lifestream currents shifted."

"You check it out already?"

"Not like I can do a full-scale survey, but yeah."

Barret was at a loss for words. *So the planet's telling us no more mako.*

"Now, maybe we could throw together a mako reactor in some other place. But first we'd hafta find the right location. Then there's the matter of transportin' all the materials and machinery in the first place. And given the lack of public enthusiasm for mako refinin' previously mentioned, well..." Cid shrugged.

"Damn. Always kinda assumed we had the option."

"When the reserves run out, it'll be the end of the mako age. The world's gonna step backward all the way to the age of coal. We'll just have to poke along in the good ol' steam wagons again. Go back to the chocobos-are-the-fastest-form-a'-ground-transportation-thank-you-ma'am era. Not that that's so bad, really."

"So we're just gonna give up and live life goin' backward?" Barret protested. "Sure, we screwed up. Big-time. An' maybe tryin' to get back on the same track ain't the right idea. But are we just gonna stop trying? Raise our hands and say screw it?"

"Not necessarily. We still got oil," Cid said with a grin.

"That useless goop?" To Barret, who worked and grew up in a coal miners' town, the mention of oil was a surprise. All it was ever good for was burning in lamps.

"Useless? Nah. It only seemed that way compared to mako. But back in the day, oil was gonna fuel the modern age," Cid replied. "They were even developin' ways to refine it into different kinds of fuel. Then mako came along, and all those same engineers dropped oil like it was yesterday's girl to line up for a dance with the new belle of the ball."

And oil became a footnote in history.

"But it's still around. Shinra figured it could be worth somethin' someday, and they even drilled for it. Problem is, the well Shinra built was out offshore, on the seabed…"

"Could you reach it by sub?"

"Not without mako to fuel it, we couldn't. Besides, the Lifestream smashed up the pipeline."

"So you don't have oil any more than you've got mako."

"I didn't say that."

Cid continued, explaining how he and his team had pulled out old records and located a pre-mako oil field. Luckily, it wasn't too far from Rocket Town. At the site, they'd found drilling rigs and a refinery that could turn the oil into gasoline—half-ruined, to be sure, but there nonetheless. Cid and his companions rebuilt the facilities and had been operating them even while they built the airship. However, gasoline didn't yield enough energy, so they had been working on developing a more potent fuel. Recently, they had hit upon a formulation that burned faster and released more energy than any gasoline. Jet fuel. Problem was, they also needed to build an engine that could handle it—and that was proving harder than they thought.

"That's amazing, Cid! Goddamn amazing!"

"Like I said, we had the records. We didn't need any newfangled technology. Once we get that engine runnin', we're gonna have ourselves a genuine renaissance."

"I guess this means the end of coal, don't it? For a second time." Barret, remembering his hometown, had mixed feelings about that.

"Well, times change. We just happened to be born at the right moment to see it happen," said Cid.

"Dunno how I feel about that."

"Lucky, is how you oughta feel! We're living at the end of one age and the start of a new one, and we get to choose how it's gonna go down."

"Maybe."

"The only unlucky part is…"

"What?"

"With so much new cool stuff to try, no way we're gonna have enough time to do it all. Ain't that a bitch?"

Cid and Barret hiked east of Rocket Town for almost a full day before they reached the oil field where Shera was working.

"Yo!" Barret exclaimed, unabashedly glad to see her. Shera looked like she hadn't changed a lick—until he saw the signs of geostigma on her hand. Noticing his stricken look, she tried to hide her hands in her sleeves.

"Well, does it hurt?" Cid asked, blunt and gruff. "Don't push yourself too hard."

"No way we're gonna have enough time." Cid's words.

Cid looked up at the derrick. It didn't seem to be operating.

"What's the problem?"

"We shut down this morning," Shera explained. "There might be more oil in the reservoir, but yields are down to ten percent of what we started with. So we had to stop the pump."

Cid slumped and muttered, "The first day, it came spurtin' out even without the damn pump. We turned jet-black from all the oil rainin' down. Laughed our asses off."

Barret let out a heavy sigh.

"The planet ain't gonna give us nothin' for free, huh?"

"That's not true," Shera said firmly. "It's given us so much already. Coal, oil, even mako—they're all gifts. And there might be other resources we don't yet know about. We'll be okay, if we use them right. If we don't get too greedy. If we figure out new ways to do things. The planet would never abandon us. It cares. After all, the Lifestream coursing through it is made up of all the lives of people who lived on its surface."

She'll always be concerned about Cid, whether she lives or returns to the planet, thought Barret. *She cares about other people. Same goes for Cid. And me.*

"Shera...," Cid managed to say, then trailed off.

A few moments passed, and he spoke again.

"Shera. What about the fuel?"

"It's good. There should be enough for one trip around the planet, depending on engine efficiency. More than enough for a test flight, I'd say. How's the ship coming along?"

"She's just about ready, except for the damn engine. I can't get it to work, can't even see *how* to make it work. So look, Shera..."

"What is it?"

But Cid fell silent again. Barret found himself speaking for him.

"Cid wants you to help with the engine. Kick his ass into gear and keep his nose to the grindstone. You got fuel, but that don't mean the work's all done, yeah?"

"I know," said Shera, looking at Cid. "I've no intention of stopping now."

Barret wasn't finished. "And once the engine's done, there'll still be a million more things to do."

Shera only smiled.

They stood together in silence, gazing up at the derrick.

"Barret," said Cid, low and quiet. "You think there's any more oil around?"

"Tell you what. If there is, I'll find it."

Even as he said it, he could feel his doubts leaving him.

Hey, planet. Hey, all you lives pulsing through it. If you're gonna punish me, go ahead—take your shots. But I'm gonna fight back with everything I got. The only ones who get to punish me are the folk who're still alive. I'm gonna keep on living, to make sure there's a future for all of us.

When Barret came back to the workshop, Old Man Sakaki showed him a new prosthetic made just as Barret had ordered. It was carved from wood and had a warm, organic feel. Nothing like metal. And it would fit directly to his arm, no adapter needed.

Barret looked at the new hand, then at the old-timer. "Man, I feel bad. You went to a lotta trouble to make this for me—but I'm sorry; I don't need it after all. See, I gotta keep moving. I'm on a search for oil. It might take me places nobody's ever set foot in—untamed lands, places with who-the-hell-knows what kinda monsters. So I still need this damn weapon. Not just for protection, though. I'm a guy who can't stop fighting, and if I fight so somebody else doesn't have to, well, maybe I'm on the right track after all. Let's just say it's my mission... No. My penance."

Barret reckoned it was maybe the most coherent and long-winded speech he'd ever given. At least, it seemed to have an effect on Old Man Sakaki, because after hearing Barret out, he went into the back of his shop and brought out a carefully wrapped bundle.

Barret opened it to find another prosthetic, touched with rust but elaborately crafted—a steel hand with articulated fingers.

"If you practice enough, you'll even be able to write with it. Whether your writing's any good, that's up to you."

"This is more than I asked for..."

"It's payment for helping out my nephew. But since you don't seem to need it, I'll just hang on to it."

"Sorry. You must've put a lot of work into it."

"Don't worry about that. I made it years ago. Come back and get it when you're done with that mission of yours," Old Man Sakaki told him. "I'll scrub off the rust for you."

After leaving the workshop and walking awhile, Barret thought, *I shoulda written a letter to Marlene. Maybe I oughta have called her, too. No. Once this is all over, I'll come back here and write to her with that hand the old guy made, and I'll take the letter to Marlene myself.*

Suddenly, Barret wanted to scream out to the sky.

So he did.

"Look out world, 'cause here I come!"

When the Lifestream erupted from the earth, he let the planet have all those memories that no longer held any meaning. Memories of his boyhood, of his few-and-far-between friends, of battles he fought before knowing his true self, of his life in those bygone days—he let them join the rushing torrent and dash themselves against Meteor. At the same time, the core of his spirit and the feelings that bound it swept across the land, through hamlet and city alike, borne by the myriad spiraling tendrils of that great current. As the eruption caught people fleeing in panic or frozen in awe, he decided to leave his own mark. Cloud would notice, he was sure, and then he would never disappear.

So long as Cloud remembers me, I will always exist. Within the Lifestream or on the surface.

Even if his own spirit were to disperse, the merest fragment of memory would be enough. It would flow through the planet on the living stream, and then one day, with Cloud's memories to help him, he would regain himself.

FINAL FANTASY. VII

EPISODE: NANAKI

ON THE WAY TO A SMILE

Leave me be, Gilligan! I don't know what you are, but leave me be!

Nanaki, who was also known to some as Red XIII, howled at the moon, trying to spit out the tar-black creature nestled in his heart. His voice echoed out from the mesa on which he stood through the cold night air. The flames at the end of his twitching tail illuminated his shivering form and made his red fur glow.

There was no answering cry to his howl. There never was, but this time, it seemed that the silence itself was a sort of reply. *I must deal with this by myself. Gilligan resides within me. He is my enemy and mine alone.*

He'd become aware of the creature only a few short days ago. Now Nanaki tried to follow the train of events that led to the birth of Gilligan and of it taking hold inside him.

Nanaki had returned home to Cosmo Canyon after his long adventure with Cloud and the others that culminated in the defeat of Sephiroth and the saving of the planet. The people there, his tribe, celebrated his triumphant return, hailed him as a hero, and bestowed many honors upon him. They demanded he recount his adventures and hung on every word of the telling. Pride, or something like it, filled his breast.

He also told his story to his father, Seto. His own father's tale, he now knew, was not that of a coward but of a brave warrior, who to this day watched over the village from where he had been turned to stone in battle with the Gi tribe.

"Ah, Father. You and Mother were true warriors who fought to protect our village. I've tried to protect it, too, in my own way. And I think I have. But now it is time for another journey. A peaceful one this time. This world teems with life, and I yearn to see it. I want to see chocobos hatch, to see tundra turn brown, to see...to see everything.

"Grandfather told me that must be my mission, to see with my eyes and hear with my ears and remember everything, and then pass on all that I experience. It feels right to me, this new mission." Gazing up at the petrified form of his father, Nanaki added one more thing. "I'll return to tell you all that I learn. I promise."

After that, Nanaki informed the people of the canyon of his new mission, as given to him by his late grandfather, Bugenhagen. Of course, the tribespeople gave him their blessing, saying that it was a journey worth taking and that they would always be here whenever he saw fit to come home again.

As he climbed down the steep slope from the village, he turned around one more time. His people were still waving to him. In reply, he sat back and pawed the air with his front legs, and he howled into the dry desert air. *Farewell. I will return. Prosper and be safe.*

Content in the knowledge that they understood the meaning of his parting howl, Nanaki leaped nimbly down the sandstone cliffs to a spot where a small boulder sat, just large enough for him to stand atop it. He always stopped briefly here when he left the village, for one last look at the mesa upon which it stood. Beyond this point, it would be hidden from view for good. But this time, when he looked up, he found that his last view of the village was blocked by a fall of huge boulders.

The Lifestream, Nanaki realized. *Here, too, it wrought destruction, and it knocked those boulders from the rocky cliff.*

Indeed, he had seen many changes in the familiar landscape when he first came home. Now, looking around again, he saw layers of rock that had stood for ages caved in and collapsed, and prominent outcroppings that had once served as landmarks crumbled and fallen.

Nothing for it, he thought. *It matters not if some rocks are here instead of there. It's nothing at all compared to places like Midgar and other cities that have been smashed beyond repair.*

Nanaki hopped down from his boulder and set off once more. Suddenly, he sensed something. There was a change inside him. In his body—no, in his mind, his heart. He stopped short and closed his eyes, searching within.

There. That's it. What is it?

He needed to describe it to himself with words. Putting words to things helped one understand them. At least, it did for him.

It's…pitch-black. Like a hole opened up in my heart. No—not a hole. There's no emptiness. It's the opposite. Feelings, thoughts, too densely crammed together. I can feel it shaking violently. It's…transforming. But into what?

Just asking the question made him shiver in terror.

He was trembling so hard, he could barely open his mouth to breathe. He clenched his teeth and waited for it to pass. It didn't. He couldn't endure this. He gasped a ragged breath and dashed back up the steep slope toward the village.

The people who had only just seen him off gathered around in concern. "Nanaki, what's wrong?"

"Uh…" was all that came out. The dark mass that had terrified him was already gone.

"You're homesick already?" someone ribbed. Others laughed.

"I… I don't know."

"Aw, Nanaki, chin up! What happened to our brave warrior?"

"He is unchanged. I think."

Nanaki stayed and talked for a while. Then he bid farewell and set out once more. He could have taken a different path out of the village, but he made himself go the same way. He had to see if the terror was tied to that place. But nothing happened this time.

He gave a name to the terrible *thing* that had arisen so suddenly in his heart. Gilligan, he called it. There was no meaning to the name, but this way, he hoped, he would know it better. It would stop him from forgetting how it felt, how it *was*.

As Nanaki continued his journey, he tried to bring Gilligan back to mind and pore over the memory, to see if he could understand what it was. But the terror grew within him too quickly, and he had to put it away again, back into a corner of his mind. He would leave it there until he could face it with a clear head, without fear.

Nanaki left Cosmo Canyon with only a rough idea of where his travels would lead. He wanted to go west first and visit the narrow island where Yuffie's homeland of Wutai lay. Then, to the larger continent to the east. There stood Rocket Town, where Cid lived, and Barret's village of Corel, and Nibelheim, Cloud and Tifa's hometown. After that, north. He wanted to see the farthest reaches of the hinterlands, beyond the roads traveled by man.

How long it would take him, he did not know. But he was in no hurry. If it was true what they told him, that his kind could live for five hundred years, or even a thousand, then he had many human life spans to spend on his roaming.

"I will be careful. I have much to see and no intention of being killed out there."

Nanaki headed for Wutai. He hoped to find Yuffie there. The girl sometimes treated him like a pet more than a comrade, but he knew that it was just her way, and she liked and respected him.

She's like an open book, Yuffie is, her thoughts writ clear. She lacks all guile, he thought. Surrounded by people older than her, she was always striving to be on equal footing with them, determined to show that she belonged there with them in any battle, no matter her inexperience. Nanaki well understood her feelings. Though Nanaki was nearly fifty years old himself, Yuffie, a girl of fifteen or sixteen, was the one companion he had empathized with the most. His grandfather had claimed Nanaki was still a child, when his years were measured against the life span of his own species, and perhaps the old man had the right of it. He did not like the idea that he was still just a callow youth, but the fact was that he grew at a different pace than humans did, and there was nothing he could do about *that*.

By coincidence, Yuffie was the very first person he saw as he approached Wutai. He was coming over the mountains and spotted her in the distance. In his excitement, his first instinct was to pounce on her and give her a good scare, but when he looked more closely, he saw that she was dragging a boy about her age by the arms, stumbling backward toward Wutai. It looked like she had been at it for a while. The pair left a trail of something in the grass as they passed, a dark smear that stretched a long way behind them. Was the boy injured? From where he stood, it looked as if Yuffie was talking to him. She stopped, stooped over to catch her breath. Then she tried to hoist the boy onto her back, but he was larger than she was, and she staggered under the effort.

"Guess I arrived at the right time," Nanaki said to no one in particular, and he loped down toward her. He was worried for Yuffie and her friend, but he was selfishly glad for the opportunity to help someone when they weren't expecting it. He padded softly up. She was still wrestling with the unconscious boy and hadn't noticed him.

"You look as if you need help."

The boy was called Yuri, and he was sick with the same illness that was ravaging Midgar. The symptoms included dark bruising that seeped with black pus, and in many cases, the victims died soon after contracting it. It was a terrible disease, and in Midgar, it was a problem at least as urgent as the reconstruction of the ruined city, perhaps even more so.

Nanaki had heard rumors that it was contagious, but Yuffie did not shy from touching Yuri as she tried to look after him. He grew nervous. *Should I warn her?* But from what Yuffie had told him already, she clearly knew about the illness. So did she just not care? Was she willing to die?

No. That was not Yuffie's way. She wasn't reckless, and certainly not suicidal. She cared for others. Nanaki didn't know how close Yuffie and Yuri were, but he knew she would never abandon a friend.

As soon as that occurred to him, he began to resent Yuri. How dare he risk infecting Yuffie? How dare he allow himself to depend on her kindness? It made Nanaki's fur bristle. But there was nothing he could do about it. The boy was still Yuffie's friend, and she cared for him. Still, when Yuffie brought up the possibility that some materia or other might cure the disease, Nanaki scoffed before she could finish and informed her that it would never work. It was spiteful, but he could not help himself.

Yuffie scolded him for his callousness, which he had expected. What he didn't expect was the hurt and sadness in her eyes. Nanaki felt horrible.

Eventually, the three of them reached Wutai, and Nanaki decided to stay for a few days. Yuffie nursed the boy, who was quarantined with others suffering the disease. Nanaki tried to help, doing the simple tasks that were asked of him, but mostly, he just watched and observed. He wanted to commit this disease and its awful progress to memory, as another part of the process of life.

"Say, is it true you can talk?" asked one of the patients.

"Yes," Nanaki replied.

"Now, isn't that strange? Wonder why the gods made a creature like you. It's like they put a mind and heart in the wrong body. Don't you wish you were human?"

"No."

Thinking back on this exchange later, he had an epiphany. He had been given the ability to think and feel like a human so that he could understand them better. His purpose was to watch and remember the changes they underwent, to witness the rise and fall of their civilizations, and to pass down the flame of that knowledge to their grandchildren's grandchildren.

There, Nanaki thought. *That's one more thing I've come to understand.*

He wanted to linger in Wutai to observe the sick and spend time with Yuffie, but Yuffie had something else in mind for him. She asked him to leave Wutai and learn more about the disease.

So as simply as that, he left. As he descended into a valley, he turned back for one more look at the town. He hoped to catch a glimpse of Yuffie working next to the makeshift hospital, but he had traveled farther down the slope than he'd thought, and the town was already out of view.

Well, I'll be back soon enough, he thought as he set out once more—and felt something clench at his heart. *Gilligan.* It was back.

Nanaki focused on the presence within him. *This time, I'll figure out what it is.* The clump of blackness quivered, and then images started to rise to the surface. They were the faces of the people of Cosmo Canyon. They had peaceful expressions as they rose and then sank back into the void. Then a different face. He recognized it, vaguely. *Who is that?* He couldn't remember. He began to tremble all over, so hard he was unable to stay on his feet and had to lie down. *The name, you know that name. Just remember it*, he told himself. Then Gilligan showed him Yuffie's face, wearing a mild expression he'd never seen on her in real life. Her face, too, fell away into the black.

Suddenly, the idea of death came into his mind. Were the people of the canyon going to die? Was Yuffie going to die? Terror gripped him.

"Help me!" Nanaki crouched on the ground, entreating the planet beneath to hold him, to cradle his shuddering body. He was about to cry out again, hoping Yuffie might hear, when, as suddenly as it had come, Gilligan disappeared.

Gingerly, he got to his feet and looked around. He ran back up the slope of the basin to look at Wutai. He could see Yuffie, hard at work.

Long before he would, she would grow old and die. There were many elders among the canyon people, and they would go even sooner. Just thinking of it filled him with sorrow. There would be much weeping and grieving in his future; that much was certain. But why did Gilligan strike such paralyzing dread in him when it made him think of their deaths?

Was that the meaning of Gilligan? Was it the embodiment of his fear of the day when everyone he knew would be dead and gone? Nanaki shook his head, trying to clear the baleful thoughts from his mind. Of course, he understood that the death of his friends was inevitable—but he didn't want to dwell on it any more than he had to.

Nanaki changed his plan for the journey. He had a new task to find out more about what Yuffie and the others were calling the "Midgar pox."

It seemed logical to go to Midgar first. There would be as much chaos as knowledge in the city, but introspective Cloud and sensible Tifa were there, too. Given enough time, he was sure to learn something, Nanaki thought. So he headed east.

As he passed south of Mount Nibel, Nanaki entered a forest he hadn't even known was there. He soon became lost. At first, he forged ahead, trusting his animal instincts, but the forest was larger than he'd thought.

Still, he was not worried. He knew he'd find a way out. No matter how dense the foliage, he could still tell where the sun was in the sky. He set a direction based on its position, using knowledge he had learned from humans, and pushed on. Eventually, he was sure, he would emerge from the east edge of the forest.

Suddenly, he heard a gunshot. It echoed among the trees, making it hard to pinpoint the source, but he took a guess, charged forward, and burst into a clearing to find a monster rearing over a boy of about ten. The monster looked like a bear with a long tail—or maybe it *was* a bear. Whatever it was, he could see blood matting the rust-colored fur on one of its front legs...

The boy must have hit the monster with his shot, but now he was on the ground, cowering as the wounded beast snarled at him. *Now what shall I do with you?* it seemed to be thinking. Then, eyes burning red with rage, it started to close in on the boy.

Nanaki jumped from his hiding spot, grabbed the boy's collar in his teeth, and dragged him to the edge of the clearing. Then he stepped over the boy and faced the bear creature, which seemed unperturbed by the arrival of a new foe. It leaped at Nanaki, its jagged claws bared. *If those get me, I'll be in a bad way*, he thought.

"It's a Nibi bear! Go for its throat! That's its weak point!" gasped the boy.

Nanaki had no idea if the boy knew what he was talking about, but the throat was a vulnerability for many creatures, and the advice seemed sound enough. He let out a vicious, feral growl, a sound he hadn't made in a long time, hoping to intimidate the monster. The Nibi bear froze, realizing it had never encountered an enemy like this before, and warily sized him up. They glared at each other.

"What are you waiting for, Red? Do it!"

Who are you to shout orders? Nanaki thought. *This is a battle between two beasts, with no weapons but those nature has given them. It is not for humans to give commands here. The forest belongs to the wild creatures.*

Then another gunshot rang out. Blood gushed from the Nibi bear's throat, and it toppled slowly to the forest floor with a mighty *thud*. Another person—a man this time, and undoubtedly a hunter—stepped out of the trees and strode up to the bear. He fired a mercy shot into the bear's head, and the beast died with a last shuddering breath.

Then the hunter turned his gun on Nanaki. He was wary and alert, but it didn't look like he meant to fire quite yet.

"Dad, don't shoot him. Red saved me. The gods must've sent him to be my guardian! Can we take him home?" the boy cried, jumping in front of Nanaki.

"Red? You've already named him?" asked the hunter.

"Yeah. I mean, look at his fur."

Nanaki cared not at all for the name. It reminded him of his previous name, given to him by a madman. He growled his displeasure. The hunter and his son warily stepped back.

"I know what you are. You can speak, can't you?" The hunter still hadn't lowered his gun. "Shinra put out a bounty a while back for an animal, and shoot me down if you don't match the description exactly. An enormous wolf, red fur, flame at the end of the tail. Goddamn! If I'd found you a couple of years back, we'd be livin' real easy now."

"Wait. Red can talk?"

Of course I can talk. And I'm probably smarter than either of you. But I shall not talk to you. Not to a man who points a gun at me or a boy who names me without leave. I won't be your friend. Nanaki turned and darted back into the forest.

"Dammit!"

The hunter fired, but the shot only grazed Nanaki's ear. *So you are willing to shoot me after all. You're the sort of humans who would shackle me and keep me in a cage. You'd talk at me, and never listen, and imagine somehow that we are companions, that my loyalty is given and not coerced.*

After he had put some distance between himself and the clearing and made sure the hunting duo did not follow him, Nanaki stealthily doubled back to spy on them. They were still in the clearing, butchering the bear with long hunting knives.

"Dad, I wanted to keep Red."

"I guess it could've made us some money. Shinra's probably not interested in coughin' up bounties no more, but we could've made some gil chargin' people to see it. Like down Gold Saucer way, maybe."

"No, Dad, I wanted to be his *friend*."

"Don't be a damn fool." The hunter deftly severed the Nibi bear's tail. "That thing's not a pet. You couldn't ever control a wild animal like that."

Neither could you, Nanaki thought.

"All right. Let's head back and fetch more folk," the hunter said.

"Why?"

"Dammit, son, you're bein' dense today. We need help haulin' all this meat. Time was, we'd just take the tail and sell it to Shinra. They use it to make a stimulant or somethin' for the soldiers, and they pay handsomely for it. But these days, we need meat as much as we need gil. Bear meat ain't the tenderest, but it makes a decent stew when you cook it right."

"This'll be the first time for me eating bear!"

"Won't be your last. Lean times are comin', son. People're gonna get hungry, and I don't know how long it'll last. But we'll get our chances to strike it rich, s'long as we keep our eyes open."

Then the father and son departed, leaving what was left of the Nibi bear's carcass.

The hunter isn't a bad person really, Nanaki thought. *He's just doing what he can to make sure his family survives. If the Nibi bear provides meat for humans, then it is only natural for them to hunt it. All creatures must eat in order to survive.*

Bugenhagen had once told him that the difference between animals and monsters was what they did with their kills. An animal would feed, but a monster would simply kill and look for more victims. If humans were judged by the same standards, Nanaki thought, as many would be called monsters as animals.

Killing the Nibi bear only for its tail would make the hunter a monster. Killing it because he needed to feed his people made him part of the natural world. Firearms and other man-made weapons tilted the balance unfairly in favor of humans, but the food chain was what it was.

Even if I don't like them, it is not my place to stop the hunter and his son, Nanaki had to conclude.

Having grown up in the company of humans, he himself hardly ever hunted. The few times he had done it were only to assure himself that he could. The prey he had brought down died not to feed him but to test his mettle. So he was a monster, too, and had no right to judge the hunter and his son.

Most humans lived their lives with hardly a passing thought for those of the animals they consumed. Indeed, they tried very hard not to think about it and left the burden of rearing and slaughtering and butchering to others so that their own hands stayed clean, or so they fooled themselves. *And I am no different*, thought Nanaki.

But what is the point of sitting here in this clearing, brooding over such things? Perhaps there is an answer out there, a path of absolute good waiting to be found. But if it exists, I shall not find it by this bear's body.

Insects and small scavengers were already crawling over the carcass. Nanaki sat up straight and watched. Here was another part of life at work. He must quiet his emotions, observe without judgment, and remember.

"Kreee!"

With keening cries, two Nibi bear cubs came crashing out of the undergrowth, scattering the scavenging animals. They rubbed up against the carcass, pawing and nosing. *Is the dead bear their mother?* They were trying to wake her. Nanaki stared, unable to do anything—but then he remembered what the hunter had said. He would be back soon, with more men from the village. And then the cubs would be in danger, too.

If Nanaki had meant only to observe, the appearance of the cubs changed his mind. He emerged from the brush slowly, so as not to alarm them.

"She is gone. You can do nothing, and it's not safe to stay here. You must go."

He tried to urge them back into the forest, but of course, they couldn't understand him. They stared at him with uncomprehending eyes.

"You can't be here. There are more humans coming." Nanaki considered it for a moment, then sprang at one of the cubs and picked it up by the scruff of the neck.

"*Kree!*" the cub shrieked. The other squealed in reply.

This should work, Nanaki thought as he took the cub into the forest. Its sibling followed. "That's right. Keep up. Stay close to me."

Carrying the one cub in his mouth, he loped deeper and deeper into the forest. Occasionally, he had to wait for the other as it scrambled after him on its short legs, and when it caught up, he pushed on again. Eventually, he reached another open space in the middle of the forest. The ground was set with weathered paving stones—clearly, humans had been here at one time. He investigated the surroundings and found a pile of stone blocks. Perhaps someone had intended to build a cottage here. But there were no other signs of activity. Just the serene desolation of a ruin long abandoned.

Nanaki felt safe enough to set down the cub in his jaws. But when he did, it just lay on the stone, unmoving. Dismayed, Nanaki bent his head to nuzzle the little creature and, to his relief, heard soft, slow breathing. It had dozed off. *What a carefree little thing you are.*

Its brother came bounding up with another "Kree!" and sniffed his sleepy sibling, nosing it all over, perhaps intrigued by Nanaki's scent on its fur.

Curiosity satisfied, the cub yawned and snuggled up to its sibling for a nap.

Nanaki smiled indulgently at the pair. But then he began to worry. *Now what do I do? It would appear I've made myself responsible for them.*

He lay down and gazed at the sleeping cubs. Could they survive without their mother? What did Nibi bears eat? They had the appearance of fierce predators, but appearances could be deceiving. Many bearlike creatures were omnivores that relied on berries and roots for food. Nanaki himself was an omnivore, for that matter. If the cubs were, too, then it should make it easy for them to find food here in the forest.

He had to make a decision. *I'll collect some berries and tubers for them and leave. Their future might be uncertain, but I can't stay and take care of them forever. Better for them that I leave quickly, before they grow attached to me. But first...* Nanaki yawned, stretching his jaws wide, and closed his eyes. He needed sleep, too.

When he woke a little while later, the cubs were nowhere in sight. *Ah, good. They've left of their own accord. Be well, little ones.*

But no sooner did he think this than he felt something tickling his flank. He looked down to see the two cubs fast asleep, nestled contentedly against his belly.

"Ah. Spoke too soon."

Nanaki grew aware of an emotion he'd never felt before, which suddenly swelled up in his chest, too strong to be brushed aside by reason. He knew then that he would stay and care for the cubs until he was sure they could survive on their own.

Baz and Lin followed Nanaki everywhere, and he taught them to hunt. It was not his strong suit, but he worked to improve so he could pass on the knowledge to the cubs. He felt no guilt for the lives he took. This was a battle for survival, as it should be.

Sometimes, they would encounter other Nibi bears. He tried to communicate to them that he was not their enemy, but his appeals were soundly rebuffed. Each time, he was plagued with doubts anew. *I shouldn't be here; I should have left the cubs with the other bears. But there is still a chance they will accept me as a fellow denizen of this place.*

He thought of many things during his time in the forest. Each day brought new discoveries and new worries, too. But on the whole, it was a time of true peace for him. The question of how long he should keep living this way crossed his mind on occasion, and when it did, he reminded himself that it was part of his mission. And yet, at the same time, he was aware that he had come to love this life. It was hard to walk away.

Occasionally, he saw human hunters traveling through the forest in search of game. Indeed, over time he saw more and more of them, armed with weapons clearly meant for taking down large quarry such as bears. So more people were turning to bear meat as a source of food. Nanaki realized he would have to teach Baz and Lin how to evade humans, as well as how to hunt.

Months passed; he did not know how many. He had left calendars and other trappings of human civilization behind when he entered the forest. Nanaki could live either way, as a human or as an animal, and this was animal time. He had not forgotten his promise to Yuffie, and it nagged at him sometimes, but the disease was a human problem. It had nothing to do with the beasts of the forest. It sounded harsh, put into such words, but it was the truth nonetheless. When he returned to the human world, he would explain it to them: *I lived as a beast of the deep forest. My feelings were those of creatures of the wild, not of a man living in a city.*

Gilligan was still with him and appeared a few times. It had added the faces of Baz and Lin to its nightmarish visions. When their images rose out of the blackness and then sunk into it again, Nanaki shrank and whimpered in fear. But the real Baz and Lin were never far away, and when he saw and heard and smelled them, the fear thinned and vanished like the morning mist. By now, Nanaki understood what Gilligan was. It was his fear of loss. It was the terror of losing those he loved that made him shiver. This understanding made him no longer fear Gilligan. If he allowed himself to be cowed by the idea of loss, he would never gain anything in life at all.

His time in the forest came to a swift and sudden end.

Baz and Lin had been growing more independent, and they had taken to leaving his side for longer and longer stretches. Then one night, when the tops of their ears were level with Nanaki's own shoulders, the cubs simply wandered off alone and went to build their own beds of branches. *So something has ended*, Nanaki thought. It made him lonely, but of course, they had to grow up. The next morning, when he woke, he didn't see them at all. Just as they'd decided to sleep apart, now they were hunting for food on their own.

One day, a few weeks later, he was in their clearing when a gunshot broke the forest stillness, followed by the roar of a Nibi bear. It was Baz. By now, Nanaki knew the forest intimately. He ran straight toward Baz and arrived at a familiar scene.

It was the same hunter's boy, cowering on the ground. A Nibi bear was prowling close. It was Baz, but his attention was not on the boy but on the forest beyond. Nanaki realized he was waiting for Lin. Baz reared up on his hind legs, raising his front claws high, and roared. From somewhere in the forest, Nanaki heard Lin's reply.

The boy was terrified, but he still had enough wits to scan for an escape route. And then he saw Nanaki. Hope shone in his eyes. "Red! It's me! You saved me before! Don't you remember?"

That day, Nanaki had not been able to leave the boy to his fate. But now he knew what he needed to say. "This is the forest. You and I both must obey its laws."

The boy's eyes widened in wonder to hear Nanaki speak in a human voice. In his excitement, he seemed to completely forget the danger he was in. "Okay, Red. I get you. I can handle this on my own!" The boy sprang to his feet and made a dash for the gun that Baz must have knocked from his grasp.

I wasn't trying to motivate you, damn you! Nanaki hesitated, caught off guard by the boy's reaction. The boy had the gun now. Nanaki had to do something, fast, or the boy would shoot at Baz again. But before he could move, Lin burst onto the scene.

Lin swung a mighty claw and sent the boy flying through the air. He hit the ground hard, limp and still. Nanaki turned away, horrified. But under the law of the forest, the boy had simply fought and lost. *This is the way of life here*, Nanaki told himself.

Baz and Lin began to circle the boy; they both reared up, pawed at the sky, and roared mightily. *Enough!* Nanaki leaped from the undergrowth to shield the boy from the bears.

When their claws came down, instead of falling on the boy, they raked Nanaki's back instead, tearing deep wounds.

"Kree!"

"Kree!"

They cried the same pitiful distress calls that they had the day they'd found their mother slain. They backed away, heads low.

"I'm all right. Go."

The pair of Nibi bears scrambled away through the trees, almost tripping over themselves in their confusion.

"Ugh…"

Beneath him, the boy groaned.

"Now where'd he get to? Damn half-grown fledgling thinks he can take on anything."

That had to be the father. Nanaki slinked quietly back into the undergrowth.

"Godie! Dammit, boy, what are you playin' at?!"

As the hunter ran up to his son, Nanaki was startled to see the man was not alone.

"Sounded like a Nibi bear. It must have taken a swipe at him." A young woman dressed in the uniform of the Turks took a vial from her pocket—a potion, perhaps—and knelt down to help the boy.

What is going on here? Nanaki wondered. *Is Shinra still operating? What are their agents doing in this forest? I've been away from the human world for too long. What has been happening out there?*

The hunter lifted the boy onto his back. As Nanaki watched them leave, he saw Elena take out her phone and make a call. "We found at least one. We'll come back out tomorrow and try again."

When Nanaki returned to the clearing they had made home, he found Baz and Lin pacing restlessly. But when they saw him, they ran into the trees.

"I'm not angry," he said, wearily flopping to the ground. He really wasn't, but the cuts on his back stung. He needed to rest and focus on healing. Tomorrow, the Turk would be back. It sounded like she was after the Nibi bears. He would have work to do.

He sensed Baz and Lin coming near, but he kept quiet and closed his eyes. After a bit, he could feel them licking the wounds on his back, cleaning where he could not reach himself. *Thank you, Baz. Thank you, Lin.*

Nanaki woke in the middle of the night. The pain in his back had faded to a dull throb.

He stood up, pleased with his own resilience. The two bears were nowhere to be seen. Usually, they still slept within sight of him. A creeping unease came over him as he nosed through the undergrowth, looking for them. They were gone. Nibi bears were not nocturnal; it was strange for them to be active at this hour.

He took to the forest to find them.

He thought he heard a gunshot in the distance, somewhere outside the forest. His disquiet sharpened into real fear; his fur stood on end, and his legs began to shake—suddenly, Gilligan was with him. He crouched down and trembled. It had been so long since the last bout, he had forgotten how to handle it. *What am I supposed to do again? ...Yes, Baz and Lin. When I see them, the fear stops.* But they weren't there. Gritting his teeth, Nanaki forced himself to his feet and staggered toward the forest's edge.

With his eyes fixed on the ground in front of him, he willed his body onward. The change in the scents told him he had left the forest. He raised his head and saw the ground sloped gently downward, covered in tall grass except where the hunter's path wound through it. He followed the path with his eyes and, a long way off, made out lights. A settlement. One light, the biggest of them all, danced and flickered. It was a fire, Nanaki supposed. A bonfire, maybe. He tried to focus on his senses, on the things his eyes and ears and nose took in, hoping Gilligan would go away. But it didn't work. He gathered his courage and stalked toward the light.

It was just as he had feared. In the firelight, he could see Baz and Lin. They were hanging from a thick wooden beam, strung up off the ground with a rope tied around their front legs. Their tails had been severed.

Suddenly, a calm came over Nanaki. Gilligan was gone. Trying not to look at the bears, he surveyed his surroundings. There were three cabins, lights on in each of them, laughter coming from within. The voices of men and women, celebrating something. There was no one on guard. Still, he kept from looking at where Baz and Lin hung.

Had the bears come out here to avenge their mother? He doubted that animals were capable of holding grudges. Nibi bears might well see humans as mortal enemies, but that was not a matter of individuals. Of the two species, it was only humans who indulged in revenge.

Perhaps the forest had held more influence over him than he thought, because now that he was gone from it, Nanaki was feeling that same desire for vengeance growing in his own heart.

"*Kree…,*" one of the brothers cried weakly. Nanaki was startled. *It hurts*, said that cry. Despite their size, they were still children.

Suddenly, a blackness welled up inside him. It was not Gilligan this time, but a different kind of madness that devoured his reason all the same. Rather than fighting it, he let it grow.

Inside one of the cabins, a baby cried. It was a message. *Listen. They have a baby. They are a family. Think about that baby. It has done nothing wrong. It is innocent and does not deserve your wrath. Nanaki, bite back on your anger. Keep it within.*

In the narrow space in his heart where both human and animal lived, he was being torn asunder.

A bullet thudded into the ground beside him, and at the same time, he heard the sharp retort of the gun. *Fool!* He'd forgotten the danger, so all-consuming was his rage.

He glanced over at Baz and Lin. He had imagined the cry, he realized, for both had clearly taken their last breaths some time ago. Between the half-closed lids, he could see their bright-red eyes gleaming, but it was only reflected firelight. It felt as if the flames were burning his own eyes, turning the whole scene crimson until he could see nothing at all.

Another gunshot, another kick of dirt near his legs. He had pinpointed the source now. He charged toward the nearest cabin and crashed through the glass window. He landed inside in a low crouch, prepared to spring. Several men swung their weapons toward him.

It may have been human emotion that led me here, but now I crouch before these men as a wild beast, Nanaki thought.

He could not tell the humans apart. Their faces were all the same to him.

A gunshot, and this time a sharp pain ripped his cheek. That was all he needed. Nanaki sprang at the nearest man.

What happened after that was a blur. Later, all he could remember was the pain of a bullet hitting his body and the screaming of a boy.

"I wanted to be your *friend*!"

Nanaki opened his eyes. He was lying on a wooden floor that was smeared with blood. He lifted his head to look around.

A man dressed in red sat in the corner looking at him. He knew the man.

"Think you can stand?" Vincent did not sound terribly concerned.

"What are you doing here?"

"Was going to ask you the same thing," he said indifferently.

Vincent didn't go into much detail, but Nanaki gathered that he had been on his own journey. Shrugging, Vincent said he had been "waiting for something to happen" when he noticed a Shinra helicopter fly overhead and decided to follow it to its destination, which turned out to be this hunters' settlement. When he arrived, the helicopter was parked outside, and Elena of the Turks was heading into the forest with the hunters, apparently in search of something. After a few hours, they had returned, carrying a wounded child with them. Then in the night, two Nibi bears wandered into the camp, and the hunters shot them down in great excitement. Having found whatever she came for, Elena left in the helicopter. Vincent had still been watching the village, wondering what Elena had been up to, when Nanaki appeared. Then there were gunshots, Nanaki leaped into the cabin, and Vincent figured he'd drop in and see what was happening.

"You were on top of a hunter, about to tear out his throat. The kid was screaming that you were his friend. What I saw wasn't the Nanaki I knew but a rabid dog. So I shot you."

Vincent had then chased out the hunters before they could gather their wits and start shooting him. "I gave them a good scare. In my other form."

After that, Vincent had treated the unconscious Nanaki's wounds and settled in to wait.

Nanaki looked around the room at the blood splattered on the floor. "Did I kill anyone?"

"No."

Nanaki thought, then nodded. "Good."

Nanaki lay still for a few moments while Vincent watched silently. Then he staggered to his feet to look outside.

"They took the bears when they left. Should I have stopped them?"

"No. They'll make use of them. It's the law of the forest. Or does it not count, out here in the world of men? Vincent, I'm confused. I need someone to hear what happened."

"Talk to me."

Nanaki launched into his story, telling Vincent everything that befell him from the moment he first saw the boy and the Nibi bear, to waking in this cabin with Vincent in the corner.

"What did I do wrong?"

For a long moment, Vincent said nothing. Just as Nanaki was starting to chide himself for expecting answers from the taciturn gunslinger, Vincent spoke.

"Here's what I think. You don't have any answer now, but you will eventually. Thing is, though, the answer's gonna keep changing as time passes. There's always more than one answer. You'll keep thinking about it all your life, and that's how it should be. The important thing is that you don't forget."

"Oh." This wasn't enough for Nanaki. He felt adrift, somewhere between understanding and ignorance.

"All right. Try this," Vincent added, as if he could see into Nanaki's mind. "You'll never be more wrong than when absolutely convinced you've got the right answer."

"So am I doomed to never know what I'm meant to do? No matter how much I reflect, I'll never find the right way?"

"Bingo." Vincent got to his feet, signaling an end to the conversation. "You can always do nothing at all. I've made that choice before."

"Did it work?"

"Maybe it did. At least, as atonement for my sins." With a sweep of his cape, Vincent left the cabin. Nanaki scampered after him.

Vincent started to head east but then left the road and headed into the wilderness.

"Where are you going?" asked Nanaki.

"Why do you want to know?"

"Can I go with you?"

"Why?"

"Because…"

Because I'm lonely. Because I want company. Because I don't want to be alone here, on the edge of nowhere, Nanaki thought as they walked along the bottom of a cliff the height of a city office building.

"Because of all the wrong reasons." Vincent leaped up to the top of the cliff, as light as the air itself.

"Vincent!"

But the red cape had disappeared from view, and there was no reply.

Maybe you're the one who's wrong. But even as he thought that, Nanaki realized something.

There was no point in agonizing about what was the right choice, about what he should have done. He couldn't change the past—only the future that lay ahead. What mattered was that he remembered it and kept thinking about it. That was the only way to find an answer, if there was one. If he did find one, it might help in some way. Or it might not. It was a small thing, overall, when set against the business of living and surviving each day as it came.

In the forest, none of these worries plagued me. Neither did Baz or Lin worry. They had all been happy there.

Nanaki crouched down, tucking himself close against the cliff face, and thought back on his time in the forest. He remembered the cubs and how toylike they looked in their sleep. He remembered how excited Baz became when spring first arrived. He remembered when Lin fell out of the tree. He remembered the first time they caught fish, the taste of it, and the lingering smell that the cubs could not lick off themselves, try as they might.

Nanaki was laughing as tears fell uncontrollably down his cheeks.

Farewell, world of the wild creatures.

He stood and set out to the east. Then, after a while, he changed his mind and headed north.

In Rocket Town, Cid was busy working on a new airship. But when Nanaki arrived with his half-healed wounds, Cid put down his wrench and set him up with warm food and a place to rest.

As his wounds healed, Nanaki took to watching the engineers and workers scrambling over the nearly completed airship. He was startled to discover that he had spent two years in the forest with the Nibi bears. When he reminded Cid how long it was since they had last seen each other, Cid was surprised, too. Just as Nanaki had lost himself in the forest, Cid had become consumed in his grand project, leaving no room to notice things like the passage of time.

Cid told him that Barret had stopped by, too, not so long ago. Nanaki wished he could have seen his old friend. Just as Cid did, Barret would have treated him the same as ever, he was sure.

With the airship nearing completion, Cid was in a fine mood, and he invited Nanaki on board for a test flight. Nanaki gladly accepted.

"No guarantees nothin'll go wrong, but we'll worry about that when it happens. Consider yerself warned, ol' buddy," Cid joked.

"We'll worry about that when it happens." Good words to remember, Nanaki thought.

Being in the air always made the world seem a much smaller place to Nanaki, so different from when he traveled with his own four feet squarely on the ground.

I need to thank Cid for granting me this experience, Nanaki thought. *I have hundreds of years to spend in this little world. The process of life involves so many things of which I am still unknowing. I have much to see and much to learn. Down there on the surface, standing in such a vast world, it is perfectly normal to lose one's bearings. But from here I can see it is not all that big, that it is possible to hold all of it in my mind.*

The realization lifted his spirits. The world was not infinite, after all.

"It's as if the planet is waiting for me to discover it," Nanaki murmured.

"If ya say so— Huh?" Cid interrupted himself. "Take a gander down there!"

"What is it?"

"Tan my hide if that ain't Yuffie. What's she doin' all the way out here?"

Nanaki would rather have put off seeing Yuffie again for a little while longer. He'd left her with a promise to find out more about the disease, but he'd done nothing of the sort. Still, as Cid landed the ship near her, he had to hide his reluctance and pretend to be excited to see her. Soon enough, Cid took off again, leaving Nanaki and Yuffie alone together.

Yuffie immediately assumed command and announced that he would join her in her search for materia. But Nanaki's opinion on that hadn't changed. Although he'd first blurted it out just to spite her and her friend Yuri, he believed more than ever that there was no materia in the world that could cure the Midgar pox—which, he'd just learned in Rocket Town, was now being called geostigma.

If proof were needed, he said to Yuffie, she only had to consider her own experience. She had been hunting two years for a materia cure, without uncovering anything except rumors. *If you couldn't find this miracle materia, then surely no one can. It simply doesn't exist.*

Even as he told what he thought was the truth, he saw her distress and immediately regretted it.

"But what do I know? Maybe it just needs two people searching. I'll help you look," Nanaki promised.

He went with Yuffie to a materia cave in the snowfields of the north. But they returned from the freezing cavern empty-handed.

"Ugh, fine! I'm convinced! There isn't any!" she groaned.

"You're giving up?"

"No, I'm gonna keep looking. They're counting on me."

"But you're convinced the materia doesn't exist."

"That was the last materia cave I knew about. But I could've missed something along the way, so I'll start over and search 'em all again. It hasn't been a total waste of time, by the way. I've been doing a lot of thinking, and I'm pretty sure I've got some things figured out." Yuffie gazed into the distance.

In between journeys, she had been teaching martial arts to the patients in Wutai. Just the children, at first—but later, the grown-ups, too. They enjoyed getting exercise under Yuffie's instruction, if their condition allowed.

"So, um, the sickness...I think it's got something to do with the Lifestream. But the thing is, not everyone catches it. It kind of, I don't know, gets into the cracks in your heart...like if you're depressed or in pain or you've given up on life or something. But if you're doing things, like if you're studying martial arts and moving around a lot, then you don't brood as much, right? You keep yourself busy all day and then, *bam*, at night you just wanna hit the sack, and you don't have time to overthink and make yourself all sad. It's kinda how I used to live, before all this stuff went down, and I wanna get back to that, too." She turned to Nanaki with a grin. "Whatcha think?"

"I think you're onto something."

"I know, right?" Yuffie pounced and wrapped her arms around his neck, practically strangling him.

"Hey, quit it!"

"Say, you're pretty banged up. What've you been *doing*?"

Nanaki considered his answer. "I've been...trying to find things to remember."

It was not something he'd planned, but he realized that over the course of his journey, he had thrown himself into the cycle of life and death and started living his days like he rarely had before. He was remembering things. He was gaining an understanding of things he would never have had by merely observing. The wounds on his body—and, yes, his heart— were the proof of his lessons.

"Oh, *please*. You're always trying to make everything you do sound so noble and *important*!" Yuffie squeezed him again, more carefully this time.

"Let's both give it our all, Nanaki."

After that, Nanaki returned to his journey and, in the fullness of time, visited nearly every corner of the world. When he encountered wild animals, he wondered if he might live alongside them. When he met humans, he made an effort to engage and talk with them. He felt he could come close to learning how the world truly was—regardless of what was deemed right or wrong—from these interactions. Within him, many new names came to be. Sparkle, dolly thief, shellfish, spider stream, puppy love, screaming trees—everything had a name bestowed by the wisdom of experience. Sometimes those experiences were precious, and sometimes they were painful.

Only one thing troubled him during these full, busy days, and that was the return of Gilligan. The more time he spent alone, the more the darkness seemed to grow inside him. It seemed that as he learned more, and as he acquired more experience, the more he had to lose, and it was this that made Gilligan grow.

But if Gilligan was nothing more than the fear of loss, why was he still afraid of it? If he knew its true nature, why did he still collapse to his knees and tremble in terror when it came? Why did it take longer and longer to recover each time?

After a time, he concluded that he must be mistaken about its nature. He considered again what Gilligan might be. It was something that struck a blood-chilling terror in him, that much was certain. He simply did not understand what it was that terrified him so.

"Gilligan?" Vincent said under his breath after hearing Nanaki's tale again, this time beside the spring in the Forgotten City. "I might have an idea."

"Then tell me," said Nanaki, seizing on the promise of an answer.

"Loss will come someday, and you will grieve. The thought of that terrifies you. Thing is, you'll get used to it eventually. Even if you don't think you ever could."

"Perhaps."

"Gilligan is from a future that you don't even know enough to fear."

"I don't follow."

"Try this. Imagine a time when all the people who know you, all the things you've given names to, everything you care for exists nowhere but inside you. When there's no one else to share them with."

"I'll try."

Nanaki imagined it, and as soon as the idea started to take form in his mind, Gilligan awoke inside him. He tried to quell his trembling and stay focused.

He imagined bounding up a steep hill that overlooked Midgar, reaching the top with a powerful leap, and, beyond the rise, seeing a ruined city grown over in thick foliage, buried under plants he could not name.

People still lived there, but no one he knew. If he went down and talked to them, someone might listen, intrigued and impressed by the tales he had to tell. But no one would reply, *Ah yes, I remember those days*.

"I'll be alone," he whispered with a shudder. "I'll outlive everyone I know. I'm afraid of how lonely I'll feel. Is that Gilligan? That fear?"

"I'd call it giving up on the game before you've played it through."

"Who's giving up?" Nanaki snarled.

Vincent only snorted at his anger. "You ever tried imagining a brighter future, one where you aren't alone? Hell, maybe one where you have kids?"

"Kids? Me? Closest I've ever come was a pair of Nibi bears."

"All right then, how about this: Once every year, you come to Midgar. I'll meet you here, listen to your dumb stories, and look completely uninterested."

Nanaki tried imagining that very scene. Vincent's apathetic face was right in front of him now. His trembling stopped. Gilligan was leaving.

"You've stopped shaking."

"Yes, but, Vincent—someday even you will…"

"Nope. Not me. I don't age, and I don't die. It's…a mixed blessing."

"Oh."

Nanaki thought of the loneliness Vincent would have to endure. Nanaki's kind had a long life span, but he would die one day. Measured against immortality, his life was but a blink of an eye…

"Well, all right. I'll come and visit you. As often as I can."

Vincent watched Nanaki with a complicated expression and finally said, "Let's keep it to once a year. Don't ask me for more than that."

"Why not?"

"You're annoying." Vincent looked away, hiding his face in the collar of his cape, and there was a slight tremble in his shoulders.

Was Vincent actually chuckling?

"Gilligan. Really, *Gilligan*?"

"Hmph. Laugh if you want."

"Don't mind if I do." Vincent laughed aloud.

Nanaki tried to look stern, but in the end, he couldn't help himself. He had to join in.

For the first time since the age of the Cetra, the Forgotten City rang with laughter.

She discovered there were many more spirits than before who resisted merging into the Lifestream's eternal flow. They were not like *him*, but she sensed the same hate, the same anger in them that led him to reject the planet and its Lifestream. She believed this was due to the influence he exerted in the living world.

Whenever such souls entered the Lifestream, she tried to relieve them of their anger. Beneath the spite and rage would be the memories of an ordinary man or woman—memories with a common person's share of hardships, to be sure, but not devoid of joys great and small. She contrived to free those memories so they could move on and melt into the stream, and soon enough, the empty shell of hate that remained would dissolve, too. She was pleased that she could help these souls, but she encountered more and more of them as time went on, and she found that she alone was not enough.

She dove into the current and rushed from here to there, seeking out spirits to help her—other Ancients not yet dispersed. The fading shards of their consciousness responded to her call. Heartbreakingly few though they were, she infused them with her memories and gained their help. Still, it wasn't enough. The pollution was spreading, gaining the upper hand.

She thought of Cloud, living on the planet's surface, in the corporeal world. If she wanted to curtail the torrent of anger flowing into the Lifestream, she would have to stop it at the source. Up there, on the ground, among the living.

Cloud will help me. I know he will. But I also know it will end up hurting him.

The Cloud she knew had a heart so very easily wounded.

FINAL FANTASY. VII

EPISODE: YUFFIE

ON THE WAY TO A SMILE

The Forgotten City. After Aerith died, they had laid her to rest there in the small spring, so when Yuffie, Cloud, and the others finally defeated Sephiroth, it seemed only natural that they return there to tell her the news.

They stood together at the edge of the water. No one spoke aloud. Instead, each told Aerith their own tale, in their own silent words.

"See you," said Vince, in his deep growl.

Yuffie turned to see only a flutter of a red cape. He was already leaving. *Seriously? Just like that, you're bailing on all of us?*

"Hey! Wait just a minute!" She ran after him. "What kind of good-bye is that? I thought we were friends."

Vincent didn't turn or even break stride. Yuffie dashed ahead and planted herself in front of him, glaring up at him, but his gaze seemed fixed on some point far in the distance. She couldn't tell what he might be thinking—only that some powerful emotion had him in its grip. In that moment, she understood that she had no means to stop him.

"Look after yourself, kid," he said as he swept past her.

Yuffie blinked at the unexpected kindness she heard in his voice, then smiled. So he *did* care, at least a little bit. She could leave it at that.

Cloud, Tifa, Barret, Cid, and Red XIII watched it unfold. "I guess he's got somewhere to be," Yuffie reported to them.

"I reckon Mystery Man's got a girl hidden away somewhere he's itchin' to see. Speaking of, it's time I took off myself," said Cid.

"Yeah. Me too," Barret agreed.

Everyone else has people they want to see, thought Yuffie. *What's wrong with that? ...Nothing.* Still, she couldn't help but protest.

"So just like that, huh?"

"Aw, shit. If we all get desperate for each other's company, we know where to find everyone." Cid was turning to go as he said it. Cloud and Tifa shrugged; Red XIII looked at the others and nodded in agreement.

Pfft. Red's just pretending he doesn't care.

"I guess so," Yuffie mumbled.

It still didn't sit right with her, but in the end, what could she do?

"Guess we'll go, too."

Cloud and Tifa started walking away.

Darn it. This is good-bye for real, thought Yuffie. *Fine. If that's what they want, I can play along. I'll do my fond farewell, and then—*

But before she could say anything, Barret shouted, "Crap, I almost forgot!"

Sheesh. Way to butt in. Just like usual. He thinks he's like a boss or something, but he isn't. As she glared at him, Barret removed some materia from his gun arm and gave it to Cloud.

"What's this for?" said Cloud.

"Hey!" cried Yuffie, louder than she meant to, as she realized she'd forgotten the important part—the whole reason she'd joined this quest.

"If you're giving away materia, can I have it? Or, er, half of it? Or something? I'll take it back to Wutai and keep it safe. I'd hardly use any of it."

The others all looked at her, eyebrows raised. She generally liked to be the center of attention, but this was different.

She kept talking to cover up her embarrassment.

"The thing is, I was already on a quest for materia when I ran into you guys, and I kinda joined 'cause it looked like you had lots to spare and stuff and you could help me find more, and some of the stuff you have is kinda rare, so if you've got extras, I mean..."

Combining cutting-edge technology developed by Shinra and arcane lore passed down by wise figures who studied the life of the planet, materia was infused with power beyond anything found in nature.

"And I didn't know anything about what you guys were up to or where you came from. I kinda still don't, in fact. But I fought beside you all the way, right? I mean, it wasn't about the materia, in the end. I just wanted to help. You guys are my friends, and now it's all over... I mean, *c'mon*. How many times have I saved your butts?"

Even as she was saying it, she was doing a mental count and realizing the answer was: zero. *Whoops.*

"It would have been way harder without you," said Tifa.

That caught her off guard. "Huh?"

"You're strong and bright and cheerful. Just like how I wish I could be."

"What?!" Stunned, Yuffie didn't know what to say. Tifa smiled quietly at her. "Wait, do you really mean that?"

"Mm-hmm." Tifa nodded firmly.

"Um…heh, thanks." Even as she tried not to blush, Yuffie starting thinking. *Hey-ho, maybe I am gonna get lucky with the materia here.*

"What do you think, Barret?" asked Cloud.

Wait, why do you want a second opinion from him*?* Yuffie thought, but she stayed quiet and tried to keep smiling.

"Hrrrm," Barret grunted. "Yuffie's been good to have along. Ain't gonna deny that. But this materia? That's a whole other thing."

"It is *not*! It's totally related! Maybe we're done fighting Sephiroth, but I've got big, big ideas for rebuilding Wutai. It's my dream, and I need materia for it!"

"…Rebuildin'? By your little lonesome?"

That was Cid. Yuffie glared at him. *All these old guys need to stop butting in!*

"Speaking of, Midgar's havin' a helluva time right now," he continued.

"Yeah. It is." Cloud thought for a moment. "All right, Yuffie. How about this? We'll give you the materia."

"Yes!" A mental fist pump.

"But I'm going to hold on to half of it for safekeeping."

"Wh—? Hey! No fair!" Victory snatched from her grasp, Yuffie prepared for another round of protests.

"Listen. A lot of our materia is for fighting. It's not going to help you or anyone rebuild a town. I'll let you have the healing materia, but I'll hang on to the rest. Out of all of us, I'm the one who's most used to handling the dangerous stuff."

"Okay, I guess I don't really need a huge arsenal…"

"Right?"

"But it would be better to have some. You know, just in case, er, I don't know. In case monsters attack." Yuffie wasn't giving up yet.

"Tell you what. When you get back to Wutai, if you find you really need some attack materia to feel safe, give us a call. We could work something out."

Cloud sounded convincing, but Yuffie was pretty darn sure he was hidebound on keeping the materia for himself

But I guess a stash brimming with the power to wreak total havoc wouldn't actually do much for Wutai. Not now. It's not like before, when we had all those desperate battles to fight.

"Fine, I guess. But you better take good care of my stuff, okay, Cloud, or you'll be in *seriously* big trouble!"

"So there you have it. I'm the owner of the world's largest materia arsenal."

Yuffie had a captive audience in the form of the chocobo she was riding home to Wutai.

"You think maybe I should get a change of clothes somewhere? I mean, these are falling apart after all that adventuring."

She had to look smart for all the people who would surely rush to the gates to welcome her back. Everyone must have heard by now that the fall of Meteor had been averted thanks to her and a few others. Obviously, they would demand to hear stories of her daring feats.

"On the other hand, maybe I should stick with the rags. Then everyone will see how hard I fought. Yeah. That would be more impressive. Anyway, I don't have time for shopping—I need to practice describing how awesome we were!"

But then, Yuffie realized, she only really knew about the bits she had been involved in. She never thought to ask about the course of events that had brought the world to the brink of destruction.

"Crap."

How did it all get started, exactly? Whose fault was it that the world got hit by an almost-apocalypse? There was quite a lot she had missed, joining the quest in the middle.

"I really should've cornered somebody and pumped them for details. Well, whatever. It's not like anybody back home knows anything. I'll just patch something together. Sephiroth was a member of SOLDIER working for the evil Shinra Electric Power Company, and then he came up with something even more evil. Cloud and the others were chasing him and fighting Shinra at the same time. Then the royal-pain-in-the-butt Sephiroth cast some sort of über-magic called Meteor to make an asteroid crash into the planet. So we risked our lives in a massively heroic battle to stop him. Perfect. That about sums it up."

*　　*　　*

Yuffie did not know that news of recent events had already reached Wutai, and people were aware of what happened. Except for certain parts of the story. Such as, for example, the contribution of Yuffie and her friends.

"Aha!"

Wutai came into sight. She had passed by it a few times during her recent adventures, but this time, it felt different. Her quest was over, and this was a proper homecoming. Yuffie leaned forward on her chocobo and gazed over her home from afar.

"Huh? What the—?" She rubbed her cheeks with her sleeve, wiping away sudden tears. *What the heck am I crying for?*

It was early morning when Yuffie arrived at Wutai proper. She unbridled the chocobo and sent it off with a slap on its rump. She kept her head down as she scurried through the streets—she wasn't quite ready to let people know she was here yet. She ran straight for the house where her father, Godo, ought to be, thinking that while her tattered wardrobe would be more evocative when telling her amazing story, she might at least wash her face.

Thok, thok, thok. Godo was in the entryway, hammering at a post with a wooden mallet.

"Guess who?" said Yuffie, an expectant grin on her face. Godo turned to face her. "Yep. It's me. Back from my adventure. We did it."

Godo nodded gravely. "I'm glad to see you home and safe, and I hope you're done with your little excursions for a while, because our town is in trouble, and everyone has to pitch in to help. Wutai needs the strength of its young people."

With that, he shouldered what appeared to be a bag of carpentry tools and set out for the center of town.

"Hey, hold up!" Yuffie rushed after him. He was walking briskly, apparently in a hurry. "Don't you want to know all about my adventures? What about my grand welcome? Where is everyone?"

As she trotted along, trying to keep up, she gave a breathless and drastically abridged account of her adventures with her friends and how they had called upon the Lifestream to save the planet from certain doom. Godo stopped short and gave her a dubious stare.

"That sounds most exciting, to be sure. But no, we've had no news of your whereabouts. All we heard was that there was a quarrel between those idiots at Shinra and a SOLDIER fighter who lost his mind, and the entire world was plunged into chaos because of it. Finally, the cosmos grew angry and decided to put a stop to the squabble by sending Meteor to smash the planet, but the planet fought back by releasing the Lifestream to destroy Meteor. As for you and your friends…no one mentioned you," he told her, quite serious.

"The cosmos decided? That doesn't even make sense! Who told you that?"

"Well. That bit was my own interpretation, based on the events. Perhaps the truth of it lies elsewhere, but what does it matter, really?" He gave her a look. "Yuffie, if I were you, I wouldn't go around telling people you were involved, whether it's true or not. The Lifestream affected us badly here. There is a lot of anger. People are looking for scapegoats to blame for starting the whole mess in the first place."

"You gotta be kidding me!" In her frustration, Yuffie fired off a series of rapid punches at the air. *Shf-shf-shf.*

"I hope you'll channel that abundant energy of yours and use it for the good of our town."

"So what's the problem anyway? What d'ya need my help for?" She pouted, finally looking around.

She hadn't noticed when she first arrived, but many of the buildings were damaged, some more heavily than others. The red roof of the training hall that had stood for generations had partially caved in, and most of its tiles lay smashed on the ground. Staring at the rubble, Yuffie began to feel uneasy.

"What happened?"

"Wutai was in the Lifestream's path. It was a terrible night; every building in town creaked and groaned. I'm sure Midgar had a worse time of it, but the buildings here are old. There's more damage than what we can see from the outside. There are cracked pillars, broken beams, slumping walls. Even the buildings that look untouched could collapse at any moment. So I'm using this mallet to— Yuffie, are you listening?"

She was peering at the people working on the buildings, shoring up walls and repairing beams. Quite a lot of them were bruised and bandaged.

"Is everyone okay? Did people get hurt?"

"Many of us did. But thankfully, few were badly injured."

"But some were?"

"Yes, I'm sorry to say. Not everyone has recovered, and there is little you or I can do for them. Buildings, on the other hand..." Godo was holding out a second mallet he'd fished from his toolkit.

"You say we can't help the injured. But you're wrong about that." Yuffie took a healing materia from her bag and held it up to her father.

"Oh?" Godo warily narrowed his eyes. "Now, what else have you got in that bag of yours?"

"Just more of the same. I was gonna bring back a whole bunch of different materia, but... Well, you know, the fighting stuff is kinda dangerous, and I figure it's best not to keep it lying around near people's homes, right?"

"Indeed. Very wise of you."

Godo took stock of the red-roofed training hall.

"It's going to take some doing, but we should be able to get the roof back on." Then he bellowed at a group of people working nearby.

"Ho, there! All of you, come lend a hand! We need to fix this roof and make a hospital!"

Her days as a materia hunter were over for now, but Yuffie was embarking on a new career as a healer. Everyone who came to see her left grateful for her help. She still longed to tell someone about her exploits saving the planet, but seeing how the Lifestream had ravaged her hometown, she realized that the gratitude of her patients was perhaps more important than singing her own praises.

Some people's injuries were so severe that not even her materia could help them, at least not in one go. But with patience and care, she was able to make even the most badly affected people whole again. If only she had more spiritual strength, she thought. Then the healing magic would be that much more powerful.

At its essence, materia was crystallized Lifestream. And since crystals were very stable, it took a *push* to force the power out, a sort of harmonic vibration that was driven by the spiritual energy of the spellcaster. It was draining work, and having to use the materia all day exacted a toll on her psyche.

At the end of every evening, Yuffie would be unbearably fatigued and barely able to keep her eyes open. She would take down her handmade Yuffie's Clinic sign and collapse into bed in a bid to get enough sleep to recover her strength for the next day of treatments.

"Ungh…"

Maybe tomorrow she would take a day off, she thought. Go find some Ether or something. Right. Even when she was with Cloud's bunch, they had always put their quest on hold when they ran out of Ether.

Thunk, thunk…
Bang, bang…
Someone was making a terrible racket.

"*Uuuuugh,* leave me alone, wouldya! I'm tryin' to sleep!" Yuffie shouted, but then she sat up. What if it was someone coming to her with an emergency?

Thunk, thunk…
Bang, bang…
No, it was too loud for someone to just be knocking. This sounded more like… *Oh.* Like hammering.

"That should do it. You just sit tight for a while." It was her father's voice.

"Huh?" Yuffie darted to the door—but when she tried to open it, it didn't budge.

"Hey! Dad, what'd you do? The door won't open!"

"I nailed it shut. Now, I want you to ask yourself why. How dare you keep something like that to yourself? Stay in there and think about what you've done!"

Yuffie had no idea what could have warranted her being boarded into her own room for a bout of self-reflection. Was she inadvertently rude to someone? Cast the wrong materia spell on a patient?

"Dad?!"

No one answered.

"Hello? Anybody?" Her voice sounded scared and lonely.

But then she realized that, even more than being scared, she was *tired.* Her bed beckoned.

"Stupid old idiot! Once I've had some sleep, you're gonna pay."

*   *   *

Wham!

It sounded like someone kicking the wall. Yuffie opened her eyes. She felt marginally better. At least, it felt like she'd gotten a few hours' sleep this time.

"*Now* what?"

"Yuffie, you dumbass!" The voice of a young woman, maybe the same age as herself. But no one she knew.

Why was someone she didn't even know calling her a dumbass? This was all becoming way too much. Yuffie was getting mad.

"Dumbass yourself! What did I do?"

"Yuri's mum is sick because of you!"

"Sick? How is that *my* fault?"

"You brought the sickness from Midgar!"

"I don't even know what you're talking about!"

But there was no reply. Instead, she could hear a grown-up's low scolding. *Great, I bet they're telling her not to talk to me*, Yuffie thought.

Whunk!

From time to time, something hit the wall. People were throwing stones at the training hall. And this was one of Wutai's finest buildings, the pride of the town. *They hate me enough to throw things at the training hall and knock chips out of the wall*, Yuffie thought, and a lump rose in her throat.

"What did I *do*?"

She kept repeating the question to herself until the first of the morning light started seeping in through the cracks in the wall.

"Yuffie? Hey, Yuffie, are you still in there?"

What kind of stupid question is that? Yuffie thought. But the voice really did have concern in it. She crept over to the wall. "Who wants to know?"

"I'm Yuri. You probably don't remember me. We used to hang out when we were little."

Just another voice she didn't know. And she couldn't think of what this supposed childhood friend looked like, either. She could recall hearing his name, though. *"Yuri's mum is sick because of you."* It must be that Yuri.

"How's your mom? She's sick, right? Someone said it was my fault."

"She's not doing so good. No one knows what's causing it. There's black gunk oozing out of her ears, and she's in a lot of pain. It hurts just to look at her."

"Oh. That sounds awful." Yuffie hung her head as she tried not to imagine the gruesome disease.

"It is. But I don't think it's your fault."

"Huh?" She perked up at that.

"Just hold on. I'm going to get you out of here."

Creeeak. Creeeak. She could hear what sounded like nailed planks of wood being pulled off with a crowbar. Then the door opened, and a young, handsome boy with a slender nose and long hair tied back in a ponytail appeared in the doorway.

"There we go."

"Thanks."

She still didn't remember this supposed childhood friend, but he didn't have to know that.

"Yuri! It's good to see you!"

"Oh, you do remember me!"

"'Course I do."

She felt a bit guilty about lying, but she needed allies right now, which meant Yuri and nobody else in the world, practically.

"Uh-oh. There's your dad and the others. We'd better get out of here."

Yuri held out his hand, and Yuffie grabbed it before she had time to ask herself why she was letting him take the lead. He pulled her from the training hall, and they ran as fast as they could, hands still clasped.

"Yuffie! Yuffie, stop! Gods be damned, Yuri, do you want more people to get sick?!"

With her father's voice fading behind them, the pair ran out of the town and into the countryside. She immediately started to feel better. She was totally fed up with being bossed around by her old man.

Still Yuffie and Yuri ran, hand in hand the whole way. They kept going until no one was following them anymore. Then Yuri suddenly stopped short so quickly, she couldn't help but bump into him.

"This way."

Yuri set off in a new direction. Immediately, Yuffie realized why he'd stopped so suddenly—a monster was up ahead, hissing angrily. For someone like her, with plenty of experience fighting monsters, it didn't pose much of a threat, except for the poison.

Yuffie let go of Yuri's hand and prepared for combat. She didn't have a weapon on her, but her fists would do.

"Yuffie, it's poisonous!"

"I know."

Then, quite out of the blue, Yuffie was struck by a powerful sense of déjà vu. *Of course! Now I remember Yuri!*

She recalled a time when they had been playing by the Da-Chao statues, and some oversize furry bugs came flying at them. After describing in detail all the ways they could hurt them, Yuri promptly ran away. Yuffie didn't, got stung several times, and couldn't get out of bed for three days.

"I've got materia to deal with the poison."

Fwish! The monster sprang at her. Just as Yuffie was about to bat it to the ground, a compact knife flew through the air and pierced the monster through. It fell twitching, and then it was still.

Yuffie stared at Yuri as he retrieved his knife and slid it into a sheaf strapped to his forearm. Now that they had stopped running, she could see that he was outfitted for adventuring—traveling clothes, sturdy boots, bracers, and other bits of armor.

"You used to call me a scaredy-cat. Remember? But I'm not a little kid anymore."

"You did try to run away at first."

"No point taking risks if I can help it. If anything happens to me, my mom will be all alone. Let's go."

"You want to tell me where we're going? Won't your mom be worried?"

"It's just for a little while."

Yuri reached into the leather satchel slung on his back and took out a shuriken. It did not pack the same punch as the larger ones Yuffie now preferred, but it was the same traditional Wutai weapon she had used more or less since she could remember.

"Here, I brought this for you."

"Thanks." She gave the shuriken an experimental toss. It spun in the air, traced a wide arc, and returned to her. She caught it with practiced nonchalance.

"Not bad." She grinned.

"You're pretty good."

Darn right I am. I just got back from an awesome journey to save the planet. I mean, I helped summon the Lifestream! Seriously, it's about time people start acknowledging what I've done.

"Y'know, none of this has exactly been the homecoming I was expecting. Would a welcome-back party have been too much to ask?"

"I'll throw one for you sometime. How about at Turtle's Paradise?"

"Sheesh. Sounds totally epic. Not."

They sat together atop a hill from where they could see the lights of Wutai flickering in the distance. Each time Yuffie tried to start up a conversation, Yuri would look around anxiously to make sure no one was in earshot. So they sat in silence instead.

"How were things in Midgar?" Yuri asked after a while, still scanning the area for pursuers.

"A total mess. Meteor got pretty close, and the Lifestream came and pushed it away, and even before that, there'd been some explosions—oh, and a giant monster attack. I mean, I wasn't around to see *all* of it go down, but it was pretty bad."

Yeah. Even though I did help save the world, there's so much I missed.

"What about the sickness?"

"What about it? I didn't know anything about any disease or whatever. I came here, and next thing I know, my old man's nailing my door shut."

"He didn't tell you why?"

"Nope. Probably because he thinks I'm still a kid who wouldn't understand."

"I don't think so. I bet he just didn't know what to say. I didn't know what to tell my mom, either." Yuri sounded apologetic for some reason.

"How bad is it, this disease?"

"Word from Midgar is that it's usually fatal."

"Oh." Yuffie felt bad for him, but she couldn't keep from asking questions. "Why do people think it's my fault?"

"We only got news about it yesterday. A terrible disease going around in Midgar. And we knew right away that it was the same thing my mom had caught, and a bunch of other people, too. So they had a meeting or somethin' and figured you'd brought it. You're the only one who'd been in Midgar recently."

Yuri was giving her an apologetic look, but she didn't notice.

"That was their whole reasoning?! Sure, I was in Midgar, but I haven't seen your mom, and I don't even know who the other sick people are! And besides, *I'm* not sick!"

She was on her feet without realizing it, shouting. She had an urge to punch something.

"Rats carry disease, but they don't get sick."

"So now you're saying I'm a rat?"

"No, not me. It's just what the old folk were saying. And you did see the other people, actually. When you treated them at the training hall."

"So what? This is so ridiculous!"

"They got sick after that."

"It's not my fault!" Yuffie grabbed his collar. She knew Yuri wasn't to blame, but she was still angry.

"Then let's prove it," Yuri said, unruffled.

She let him go.

"Yeah. Darn right I will! There must be someone else who was in Midgar. We'll find them and call them out! Then all those idiots who accused me can come and grovel at my feet and beg for my forgiveness. Starting with old Poop-for-Brains! Oh boy. They have *no* idea who they're dealing with!" she cried, standing tall and waving her fist at the world.

"You haven't changed much. Still all about me, me, me."

That brought her up short.

"What's that supposed to mean?"

"We should be finding a cure, not someone else to blame. I bet we could, too, if we worked together."

"But..." *He has a point.* Though that still didn't do anything for the anger gnawing at her stomach.

"If you found the cure, people would *have* to revise their opinion of you. Then you'd get your apologies or whatever."

"I guess."

She considered it. What Yuri said was true, and discovering a cure would actually be the best and nicest thing to do. But she still wanted to find out who really was to blame, just to make it crystal clear it wasn't her.

"Yuffie? My mom might not have much time left. I could really use your help."

"Okay."

She could always find the culprit later.

The pair left Wutai behind them and headed south to a region known for its materia caves. Shinra had once planned to build a mako reactor there, but locals protested, and it ended up in bitter fighting. Still, the fact that Shinra chose that location for a reactor could mean only one thing—that the Lifestream flow was strong there.

Before the disaster, the region could only be reached by means of chocobos specially raised to carry riders through rough mountainous terrain. But the Lifestream eruption had transformed the landscape, and now they could get there by foot.

Yuffie being the suspected cause of the sickness was not the reason why Yuri had sought her help. Rather, it was the fact that she had been obsessed with materia since she was little.

"There's got to be a materia that can cure the Midgar pox, right?" said Yuri. That was what he'd started calling the illness.

"Maybe."

"Do you have any friends who might know for sure?" Yuri held a gleaming new cell phone out to her.

Yuffie had an idea.

"Hold on."

She took out the PHS she'd been using throughout her recent quest and…no signal. So instead, she checked the contacts for a number and dialed it with Yuri's phone. It barely had a chance to ring before someone answered.

"Hey, Tifa? It's me, your best friend, Yuffie!"

She talked to Tifa, then Cloud, but no one had yet found a materia that could cure the Midgar pox. They could only tell her how bad it was in Midgar and that no one knew how to stop it. People were dying, and everyone was afraid. They also told her that it had appeared immediately after the Lifestream stopped Meteor.

"Everyone's as clueless as we are."

"So still no cure?"

"Hey, check that out. It looks like a new cave. Let's see if there's any materia in it!"

Yuffie handed the cell phone back to Yuri. The fissure she had spotted was at the bottom of a sheer rock face. It had likely opened up when the Lifestream transformed the terrain in the area. She started to jog toward it.

They spent an hour or more in the cave, alert for the glimmer of materia. "Gah! Not even a speck."

"But this is a new cave, right? Doesn't that mean there wouldn't be any? I mean, doesn't it take time to accumulate? Why'd you pick this place anyway?" Yuri said nervously.

Yuffie hadn't really thought it out, truth be told. "Well, if, er, the Lifestream was gushing everywhere, it could've dropped some materia. Right?"

Maybe? Is that possible? Who knows?

"Sure. I guess you're the expert." There was a tremble in Yuri's voice.

Wandering around in a gloomy cave and fighting off monsters as they went wasn't exactly a whole lot of fun. Not even for Yuffie, the intrepid materia hunter.

"Hell-oooo! Materia, come out, come out, wherever you are!" she shouted in an attempt to lighten the mood. If she was jumpy in a place like this, then Yuri was surely terrified. How many times had he gone cave crawling? Zero, in all likelihood. She ought to go easy on him.

"Let's go back outside for a minute and rethink our strategy."

Even in the gloom, she could see how relieved he was.

They were heading toward the exit when they encountered a new monster. At first glance, it looked like a big mole, but the needlelike spikes all over its body and the nasty gleaming eyes marked it as something else.

"This'll be a cinch!" Yuffie boasted, hoping to encourage Yuri, and wasted no time hurling the shuriken. It struck home, but the monster countered by spitting a fireball at them. She dodged, barely, while behind her Yuri managed to leap aside in a panic. The fireball exploded on the ground between them.

"Yuri, watch it!" she called. Yuri was staring at the spot where the fireball hit.

"Swiftness upon me!" he cried.

In the same instant, the shuriken returned to Yuffie's hand like a boomerang, and she threw it again. Its spinning blades caught the monster right between the eyes, and it fell dead. Victory was theirs.

"Aw, Yuffie, I was just about to take it down."

"Waaay too slow. I could hardly believe how long you were taking," she said. She immediately regretted her harshness. "I can tell you've been training, though."

"I might be slow to react, but I can make up for it with my skills."

"Maybe. But if you're not fast, it doesn't matter. Speed is everything, whether attacking or defending. You got that?" Yuffie went up on her toes, about to make a display of her own speed, when…

"Yuffie, look out!" Yuri drew back, fear written on his face. "On the ground!"

Some kind of liquid was seeping from the depression in the ground where the monster's fireball had exploded. In the dim light, they couldn't be sure what it was—but somehow, they knew it was not normal water. Yuffie shuddered. It gave her the creeps. Like it had some kind of evil aura.

"Let's get out of here," Yuffie said, springing into a run.

Behind them, the water began to flow more heavily. It started to gush out of the ground in great spurts, climbing the walls and the roof of the cave, as if seeking a way to get outside. It flowed faster and faster, overtaking them. Heavy drops fell down from the ceiling, and the pair covered their heads with their arms as they ran. Fortunately, they had dropped markers at the junctions to show the way out, and it was not long before they reached the exit and burst out into the open air.

The landscape was bathed in moonlight, and it was far brighter out here than in the cave. Yuffie turned back to see that the water had stopped within the cave, but it still dripped from the ceiling and made the floor shiny and wet. Even out here, with the moon shining into the mouth of the cave, the water was inky black.

"I definitely don't think that stuff is water."

Yuri didn't reply. In fact, he wasn't even with her.

"Yuri!"

She hesitated for a split second, then dived back into the cave. She found him only a few steps in, collapsed on the floor. She tried to help him stand, but there was no strength in his legs. The best she could do was prop him up into a sitting position.

"Get up! Yuri, you gotta get up!"

"I can't. Just leave me, Yuffie. Or you'll…"

"Don't be a dumbass! I can't take care of your mom for you!" Yuffie grabbed him under the arms and started dragging him backward.

"It's too late," Yuri mumbled as black slime trickled from the corner of his mouth.

Somewhere between the caves and Wutai, Yuffie collapsed to the ground, exhausted. "C'mon, Yuri. Try to walk for me. If you die out here, it'll be my fault, too. Yuri runs off with Yuffie, who was just in Midgar, and then he dies of Midgar pox? I'll *never* convince them it wasn't my fault!"

"That's not why"—Yuri could get out only a few words at a time, as if it hurt to breathe—"you dragged me...all the way here..."

"Um, yeah it is."

"No. You can't...fool me......"

He faltered, unable to finish the sentence.

Alarmed, Yuffie peered at his face. *It's okay. He's still alive. I just have to get him back to his mom.* She got to her feet and put her arms under his again.

"You look as if you need help."

Surprised by the voice, Yuffie whirled around. "Red!"

"Would you mind calling me Nanaki?" said Red XIII. A little grumpily, too, she couldn't help noticing.

"What are you doing here?" she asked.

"I'm on a quest for things to remember. I've only just started, though."

Even with Yuri on his back, Nanaki loped along easily over the terrain. Yuri was draped facedown, almost like a load of clothes to be laundered, and Yuffie ran alongside them, keeping a hand on her friend so he wouldn't slip off. Nanaki told her that Wutai was the first stop in his journey, and he planned to head east from here. He'd started with Wutai because it was the westernmost point of the known world.

With a native's pride, Yuffie informed him that, actually, Wutai was the center of the world, dividing in equal halves the open seas to the west and the lands to the east.

Yuffie saw Yuri shaking and for a second feared he was going into convulsions. But when she peered at his face, she saw that he was chuckling. The black stuff had stopped coming out of his mouth.

"Nanaki, tell us a story," she whispered to him.

"Hmm…" Nanaki thought of something. "Okay. So I have a new cell phone now. When I got back to Midgar with Cloud and Tifa, there was a merchant giving away his entire stock because, according to him, more than anything, people need to be able to stay in touch in a crisis like this. Nice guy, huh? They were expensive models, too, and everyone kept telling me that my old PHS was out-of-date, so I grabbed one."

"Must be hard to use for a guy with paws. I bet it's hardly worth the effort."

"Texting is awkward, I admit. The screen has tongue smears all over it, and it's covered in saliva most of the time, which can't be good for it. I don't often envy humans, but opposable thumbs *would* be useful, I can't help thinking."

Then Nanaki had a sudden thought, and he squinted at her suspiciously.

"But why do you care how easy it is for me to use?"

"Oh, c'mon! You can barely operate it—you just said so yourself!" She planted herself squarely in front of him, and he stopped. "It would be way more useful for someone like me. So let me have it!"

She started rummaging through the gear strapped to his body.

"Are you serious? You are literally trying to rob me," protested Nanaki as Yuffie found a strap hidden in his red fur.

It seemed to encircle his neck, like a utility belt in the wrong place, and she ducked to examine it. There was a small but sturdy leather pouch attached. "Heh-heh. Gotcha."

"Yuffie, I'll never, ever forgive you for this."

"Perfect. Then you'll never forget me, either."

Nanaki seemed resigned to his phoneless fate as she crouched down and reached for the pouch.

"Yuffie, take mine," Yuri said. "I got the same one." A pause. "In Midgar."

"Wait, what? Midgar? How?"

"I was there, too."

"But then you—" Already unraveling what it meant, Yuffie entirely lost her cool. "You jerk!"

"I'm sorry. I think I brought the sickness to Wutai. And my mom caught it from me. Her friends caught it from her… And I thought, if I could just find a way to cure it…then it wouldn't matter who was to blame…"

Yuffie stared at him dumbstruck.

"Nanaki, can you let me down? Thanks."

*   *   *

They sat in the meadow, watching the tall grass waving in the breeze. Nanaki's head rested on his front paws.

Yuri confessed everything. His mother had fallen sick months ago—not with the Midgar pox but with another illness that often affected people in this region. It had been a bad case, and she grew weaker and weaker and started talking about how she was going to die. Yuri was determined to do something. He remembered Yuffie, the girl he used to play with, and how she loved hunting for materia. So he decided to go find materia for himself.

But he wasn't intrepid enough to venture alone into the hinterlands to hunt for naturally occurring materia. Instead, he went to Midgar, hoping that maybe someone in Shinra would give him some. Unfortunately, he arrived just as Meteor appeared in the sky.

Every day, he trudged up to the Shinra Building, trying to get someone to listen to his story and give him materia, but the company was in disarray, and no one had time for a bedraggled urchin from the wilderness. When he finally did manage to corner a sympathetic employee, he was told that materia was military equipment and not for sale—at least, not by Shinra.

"Then...that day came. I holed up in my hostel in the slums and rode out the Lifestream surge. The next morning, everyone topside was fleeing down to the slums, but I fought my way up anyway. I passed a lot of sick people."

The area around Shinra HQ was a disaster zone, and Yuri realized that the world had changed and he needed to return to Wutai. When he got home, his mother asked where he'd gone, and he lied and told her that he'd been to Gold Saucer for a break.

"I couldn't stand to tell her I'd gone looking for materia to cure her and came back empty-handed."

"I know the feeling." Yuffie was still steaming about him keeping his mouth shut and letting everyone blame her. But it wouldn't help to say that now.

"You know," Nanaki interrupted. "Some say that materia embodies the wisdom of the Ancients."

"Yeah, I've heard that," said Yuri.

"It could be the Ancients wouldn't have been able to cure your mother's illness, either. It may not have existed in their day. So the materia you were trying to find likely doesn't exist anyway," Nanaki mused.

"Nanaki! Why do you have to be so negative? They were really smart. I bet they totally cured it at some point."

"Then why has no one ever found the materia, then? Surely, if it truly existed, it would have turned up— Ouch!"

Yuffie flicked Nanaki hard on the end of his nose. She suspected he was right, and it made her angry.

Because if there were diseases out there that had no materia cure, then maybe there was no materia that could stop the horrible plague that made people leak black slime and die in agony.

"Sheesh, Nanaki. You can be such an ass."

"What did I do?"

They had been away from Wutai for only two days, but as they approached, they saw a new building had been hastily erected a short distance outside the town.

"What's that for? Nanaki, you're on recon!"

"Me?"

Nanaki looked nonplussed, but he loped off quickly enough when Yuffie moved to give him another flick to his nose.

"I don't think he likes it when you do that," Yuri said, chuckling.

It was good to hear him laugh. In fact, he was looking better. *If Nanaki and I can keep up this comic act, maybe Yuri will laugh until the Midgar pox goes away.*

Nanaki soon returned. "There are beds inside. About ten or so. Four of them occupied. The people in them look like they have the pox."

Yuffie and Yuri exchanged a glance.

"Yuri, get on," said Nanaki.

Yuffie took off without waiting for Yuri to climb onto Nanaki's back.

She came up to the hut and found a small window through which to peek. Just as Nanaki had reported, four sick townspeople were lying in beds.

"What is this?" She turned back to Nanaki.

"Quarantine. The townspeople believe the illness is contagious, so they're keeping the sick people away. At least, that's what it looks like."

"So they stuck them out here in the middle of nowhere?" Yuffie said, then went around in search of an entrance.

"Yuffie, wait!"

Ignoring Nanaki's protest, she went inside. "No, no, no. This is *horrible*!" she cried to no one in particular.

"Hello, Yuffie. Fancy seeing you here. But why are you so upset?" said one of the patients calmly.

Something about the woman's voice sounded familiar. Yuri's mother.

"People who are sick need to be cared for, not shoved off into some hut outside of town! It's not right!" Yuffie knew why the townspeople had done it—but she couldn't accept it.

"Come now, dear. When a contagious disease is going around, you need to quarantine people. Surely you know that," Yuri's mother replied gently.

"But—but—!" It was the only word she could muster.

"Oh, goody. They built a house just for us," said Yuri as Nanaki carried him in.

"You think this is funny?"

"Look, it's no big deal. People are afraid. What else can they do? This place will do us fine until you can figure out a cure."

Me? What if I can't find one? Yuffie wanted to ask. But instead, she pretended to be cross.

"Sheesh! Not like I needed a break or anything!"

Yuffie spent two weeks caring for the Midgar pox victims. Despite the quarantine, new patients continued to be sent out to the makeshift hospital.

One day, her father came to visit, keeping a wary distance from the hut.

"It might not be contagious after all. People are still falling sick even with the quarantine. Which would mean—well, perhaps we were too hasty. I'm sorry."

But Godo's apology did nothing to improve Yuffie's spirits. *Never mind that now! We still have to find out what's causing it,* she thought.

She told Nanaki he needed to go out into the world and try to learn more about the pox, and she ordered him to leave that very day. So far, the sickness had affected only humans, but she didn't want to take any chances. There was no need for him to linger in this diseased place.

"Hey, Yuffie, I think I've figured out something," said Yuri. "Why some people get sick and some don't."

"What's your theory?"

"Well, the people in here were either already sick, like my mom, or they got injured badly when the Lifestream hit them. They were kind of expecting to die already."

"Are you sure?"

"Yeah. I mean, we've been talking a lot here in the hut. It was the same for all of us. Me included."

"You thought you were gonna die? When?" said Yuffie, startled.

"In the cave. Remember when I fell down and I was covered in that weird water— Ohhh!"

They looked at each other.

"Could that be the source?" Yuffie blurted out.

It made sense. The water could be causing the sickness. Yuffie immediately asked all the patients if they'd drunk or bathed in water that felt strange or was darker than it should be.

She arrived at no definite conclusions. Everyone had noticed that the water tasted different since the Lifestream swept through town, but it hadn't worried them. Wutai drew its water from wells, and the water often tasted a bit odd after earthquakes, when dust and sediment would fall into the aquifers.

Some of the sick people had been struck directly by the Lifestream. Others may have drunk contaminated water and for some reason or another been expecting to die, or at least thinking about the possibility. Nothing was proven, but Yuffie felt like they were getting closer to an answer.

Yuffie and Yuri told Godo what they'd learned, and together they wrote down a short list of rules for the uninfected.

1. Be cautious of all sources of water. Try boiling all water before drinking and washing.
2. Do not think about how you are going to die.

*   *

For the next year, Yuffie alternated between staying in Wutai caring for the patients and traveling abroad in search of a cure. She tried just doing one or the other, but when she was with her patients, she fretted that she should be out searching for a cure, and when she was traveling, she worried about her patients and yearned to go back to them.

They had to build a second hut. Three children fell sick, all brothers, aged eight and six and four. It saddened Yuffie to imagine such young children thinking they were about to die, but when they told her how the youngest had fallen in the river, and the other two got swept into the current trying to help him, and that they nearly drowned—well, it was further confirmation that she and Yuri may be right.

Geostigma, the world began to call it. That strange dark water was the vector. The illness entered people's bodies when they had given up, when their will to live had failed them.

Yuri's mother was gone. Yuri still laughed and joked, as if he had sworn to himself that Yuffie would never see him without a smile.

Another year passed. Geostigma was still spreading with no cure in sight. By now, researchers and doctors around the world were coming to similar conclusions about the nature of the disease, but most laypeople still believed that infected people were contagious, so victims and their entire families often lived in deplorable conditions. Driven into such a plight, other family members had a higher chance of falling ill as well, which only made the persistent myth harder to discredit.

Yuffie was coming up on Corel when she heard a distant mechanical growl. She couldn't figure out where it was coming from until she looked up to see a huge airship drawing close. She waved. She hadn't seen the airship before—but surely, she thought, Cid had to be on board.

"Heeey! Down here!" She jumped up and down and waved frantically, but the massive airship lumbered on, apparently oblivious.

She had heard that Cid was trying to build a new machine that would run on oil rather than mako. People had been saying he'd never do it, but it looked like he'd proven them wrong. *No surprise there.*

The ship was heading west in the direction of Rocket Town. Yuffie was just thinking maybe she should head there, too, when she saw the airship coming around again. It descended a short distance away from her, far enough that she wouldn't be blown over by the turbulence created by the massive propellers. Once the ship was down, she ran up to it, waving her arm in glee.

"Hey!"

The hatch opened, and Nanaki shot out and bounded straight toward her. Yuffie spread her arms to offer a hug, but as Nanaki leaped, she thought better of it and sidestepped at the last moment.

He looking back at her reproachfully.

"Why did you dodge?"

"Sheesh, Nanaki. Look at you—you're huge. I have better things to do than get squished."

"I'm the same size as last time we met."

"Maybe you just got more ferocious looking or something."

"I suppose I'll have to take that as a compliment."

"Howdy, Yuffie!" Cid strode over, looking fit and confident. *Has he lost weight?*

"I'm guessing that's yours?" she said, nodding at the ship.

"Damn right it is! Helluva job gettin' the blasted thing off the ground, I gotta tell ya. This is her maiden test flight."

"Looks like everything's working."

"More or less. Blasted engine sucks up fuel like no one's business. Only got enough left to take her halfway 'round the world."

"Can you get more? Fuel, I mean."

"I hadta pin all my hopes on that dingbat Barret, so I ain't holdin' my breath. He's off lookin' for new oil fields. We got the drills and derricks all packed an' ready to roll the moment he hollers." Despite the professed lack of faith in Barret's abilities, Cid sounded genuinely hopeful.

"Oh, so you've seen Barret around?"

"Yup. Mopin' even more 'an usual, but I reckon maybe he's started to get his head together. Seemed happy enough when he set off, leastwise. So wanna go for a ride?"

"I'm all right, thanks."

"You turnin' me down? You're still not over that goddamn airsickness?"

As if being airsick is a choice, Yuffie thought, then decided to shoot back.

"That's right. I'm not planning on 'getting over it,' either. The great ninja Yuffie has but one completely irrelevant weakness, and that's only because idiots like you get all nervous when a woman has no weaknesses at all."

"BA-HA-HA! You needn't worry about that last bit—you've got plenty to spare!"

Dammit, she thought. *Lost again.* But she couldn't help smiling.

"Anyhoo. I ain't gonna force you on board. But take care of yourself, an' keep doin' whatever you're doin'." Cid turned to leave.

Which reminded her.

"Hey, Cid."

"What?"

"There has to be a materia that cures geostigma. Right?"

Nanaki averted his eyes when she said it.

"Depends. What do y'all think?" asked Cid, looking her right in the eye.

"I *know* there is!" Yuffie said, loud and determined.

He pointed at her and nodded firmly.

"Then you're gonna find it!" he declared. And that was his farewell.

Yeah, right, Yuffie thought, watching him walk back to the ship. *He's just saying that. He's pretending to know stuff just like old geezers always do. But...he did say what I wanted to hear.*

Soon, the engine roared, and the ship climbed into the sky. It banked toward Rocket Town and slowly dwindled into the distance.

"Oops," Nanaki muttered. "He left me behind."

"You can join me."

"Where are you headed?"

"The materia cave in the north."

Nanaki's expression was hard to read, but from the way he kept looking down or away, she could tell he wanted to say something. She jumped onto his back and leaned forward to embrace him around his neck, then grabbed her left wrist in her right hand and pulled tight so that her left arm was digging into his throat.

"Yuffie, you're choking me..."

"Speak! You've got something to tell me, so spit it out! Come on!"

"Fine, fine. Just let me go!"

She relaxed her hold.

"I want to say the same thing I said before. I think you're on a fool's quest. You can explore every last cave in the world, and you'll never find a materia cure."

Yuffie said nothing and tightened her arms again.

"That hurts!"

"Geostigma hurts more."

"Fine." Nanaki shrugged and started trotting north with Yuffie astride him.

Swaying there on Nanaki's back, she smiled to herself.

You just don't get it, my silly four-legged friend. My search is giving them hope, back in Wutai. Yuri and all the others. So I'm going to keep looking. This materia hunter isn't retiring yet!

Despite the panic and ongoing turmoil, life on the planet was returning to a normalcy of sorts. He saw something in the new spirits joining the Lifestream—the shadowy places of the heart seemed to define them. It was pleasant to him, the persistent drifting darkness, especially when he realized it was his actions aboveground that had engendered it. Perhaps he would be able to do something amusing with it. Like, for instance, turn the entire Lifestream black.

Concealed within the planet's own life force, he floated throughout the world, leaving his mark on people everywhere he found them. More and more of them with every passing day. The others found the rhythm of their lives shattered, despair taking hold in their hearts. He delighted in this, and he invited the darkness to grow and spread.

In time, another thought came to occupy him.

I want Cloud to know this is my doing. I want them all to know.

He would need a body. There were things he had to say with his own human voice, things he had to tear apart with his own hands.

I could use Mother's power. If I had just a piece of her, I could forge another body for myself.

He tried to send his spirit above to walk the surface, but nothing came of it. The planet had consumed the memories of his own form, leaving him with no image on which to anchor his consciousness.

But then he found another memory in the Lifestream that would serve, and he bound part of himself to that image. It took the form of a young man, and he felt once again how the world of the living was unbearably confined and circumscribed—nothing compared to the freedom he enjoyed as pure consciousness.

Still. He had his mission. He created two more bodies, and then there were three. The three who walked upon the planet's surface were not him, and yet, they were. Created by the force of his will alone, deviations from the order imposed by the planet, they were at once real beings and fantastical monstrosities.

He thought about the future.

As they search for Mother, my servants will meet those who knew me, and their spirits will remind me what I once was. Once I have Mother's power, I will exist fully in the living world. It will not be long now. Even if I am incomplete, it will matter not. Cloud will be there. Cloud will complete me.

FINAL FANTASY.VII

EPISODE: SHINRA

ON THE WAY TO A SMILE

Tseng, director of the Administrative Research Department of the Shinra Electric Power Company, had been on a mission to obtain the mystical artifact known as the Black Materia before Sephiroth could. The quest had taken him from one end of the planet to the other, until it led him at last to the Temple of the Ancients.

There, however, he encountered Sephiroth and was gravely wounded. He could do nothing but lie collapsed on the ground, watching his own blood spreading in a pool around him. He grew faint, and he knew it was only a matter of time before the end came. But just as he was resigning himself to die, Aerith and her friends arrived at the temple. They, too, were chasing Sephiroth.

For a long time, it had been Tseng's ongoing assignment to monitor Aerith, the last descendant of the Ancients, with the end goal of persuading her to cooperate with Shinra.

While he and his colleagues were not shy about employing violent means to get results when the situation warranted, they had learned this particular operation required a gentler touch. It was a lesson paid for dearly—the attempt to control Aerith's true mother by force had resulted in her death.

That bungled operation had left Aerith as the only living Ancient in the world. She had to be approached with the utmost caution, and Tseng, as a representative of the company's darker and more deadly side, thought he was a poor choice for the job. Uncertain how to proceed, he let weeks pass while he did nothing more than watch over her.

Funnily enough, Aerith spoke to him first. She was still a child when one day she strolled right up to him.

"Thank you," she said.

Tseng wondered if he had heard correctly.

"You're protecting me, aren't you?" she said when he didn't reply.

The misunderstanding could have worked to his advantage, as far as the mission was concerned. But instead, he told her the truth. Honesty was rarely his policy, at least professionally, but it had to be that day.

"I work for Shinra. My name is Tseng. I'd like to talk to you."

"I hate Shinra!"

Watching her small figure dash away, he felt a sense of relief. It was better this way. Even if the day came when he had to bring her in by force, he felt that the one thing he couldn't stand to do was deceive her. Strange, that.

Weeks turned to months, months to years. Aerith grew. Little changed, however, until the day she somehow fell in with the anti-Shinra organization Avalanche. That made the situation very different. Frustrated by his inability to control things, Tseng treated her with a cavalier villainy, so theatrical that his fellow operatives never let him live it down.

But every time they mentioned it, the same thought came back to him.

It isn't just theater. To Aerith, Shinra is nothing but evil. And evil is as evil does.

In the end, even when he thought he was dying, Tseng still chose to face Aerith as a Turk.

"Damn. Since I let you slip through my fingers, it's been one disaster after another."

And yet, Aerith shed tears for him. She found it hard to see him as an enemy, when she had known him since she was small. Tseng never imagined anyone might mourn him. *Maybe death will be kind to me after all*, he thought, but the words that came out were more like a joke.

"I'm not dead yet."

After she walked away, he sat there quietly waiting for the end. It seemed to take a long time. He felt his consciousness slipping away, but the telltale rush of his spirit dissolving into the Lifestream had yet to come.

Then salvation arrived in the form of Reeve. Well, actually, in the form of a ridiculous animatronic cat riding a fat moogle, which Reeve operated with a bizarre level of expertise. He called it Cait Sith, and he'd used the contraption to infiltrate Aerith's party and gather intelligence.

"Looks like you're in a bad way, Tseng," Cait Sith remarked.

"Where is the Black Materia?"

"…"

There was no reply. In fact, the robot didn't move at all. Tseng was starting to wonder if it was malfunctioning, when Reeve spoke again. "Sorry. I'm trying to operate two units at the same time. It's a little complicated."

"I see." Tseng didn't understand or care. He made himself be patient.

"So the Black Materia—I'm going to let Cloud's crew have it for now. Better that than Sephiroth getting ahold of it."

Cloud. The young man was deeply involved with all these tumultuous events, but *how* was another puzzle to which Tseng didn't have all the pieces. At the same time, it seemed inevitable that he was. Cloud was the key, Tseng felt certain—but he could scarcely imagine what kind of door that key might open.

If they wanted to prevent the activation of the ultimate black magic—Meteor, a spell with the power to destroy the world—better to let Cloud hang on to the Black Materia.

"Cloud gets the Black Materia," said Tseng. "Understood."

"And, Tseng, I'll notify HQ of your status."

"…Thank you."

"As for me—well, Cloud and the others found out I'm spying for the company, but I'm going to stay with them anyway. They're an interesting bunch. Or at least, I'm interested in them. Now, hold on—I've got to move you."

Tseng had quite a few more questions, but as the large moogle picked him up, the pain knocked him out. His recollection of what followed was hazy.

He was hoisted aboard a ship by his former superior and two former comrades. Tseng wondered why Reeve contacted them instead of regular company employees. Maybe Reeve had been in touch with them all along.

More questions arose in his mind, but Tseng didn't have the strength to ask any of them. He spent most of the journey unconscious before he finally came to in a small room on solid land. The smell of rust and brine in the air told him he was in Junon. Someone—the company? Reeve?—had arranged for a doctor. It would appear he was going to live.

＊ ＊

Much happened while Tseng was recovering. Aerith was killed, and the Black Materia passed from Cloud's hands to Sephiroth's.

Sephiroth used it to cast the terrible spell Meteor.

Reports said it would be less than a week before impact. Meteor would crash into the planet and destroy everything. Nothing could alter its course, though that didn't stop people from trying.

*   *

From Midgar's Sector Zero, near the Shinra Building, one could see the giant cannon, airlifted from Junon and now looming over Sector Eight on hastily constructed steel supports. The Sister Ray, as it was named by Scarlett, the director of Weapons Development, was their last hope of taking down Sephiroth. Specialized pipelines ran from each of Midgar's operational reactors directly to the Sister Ray, which would fire a beam of pure mako energy, amplified by Huge Materia, into the distant Northern Cave where Sephiroth still slept.

If they could destroy him, the nightmare he'd summoned would be neutralized, and Meteor would vanish from the sky. Or so they hoped.

They also hoped that with the apocalyptic threat defeated, the monsters called forth as living weapons might return to their resting places as well.

"In theory, it should work." Rude stared up at the Sister Ray.

"And in practice?" said Reno. He sounded serious, unusual for him.

"Let's just say there are some unanswered questions."

"You're telling me! I got a bunch."

"Like what?" Rude had to ask.

"Okay, check this out. Like, they're just gonna go ahead and fire it, right? Not even a test run? Is Midgar gonna get razed when the thing recoils? What if they miss? What if it sparks a chain reaction? What if it—?"

"If I tell you it'll be fine, will you shut up?" Rude rumbled.

"Sheesh, no need to get pissed off. I was just *asking.*"

The Sister Ray, which was billed as the world's savior, accomplished nothing and ended up an enormous hunk of scrap metal. All it did was incite one of the Weapons to retaliate and demolish most of the Shinra Building.

Reno and Rude were familiar enough with death and destruction. They were Turks, after all. But seeing it meted out on the Shinra Building was a different matter. As field agents, to them, headquarters was like a refuge or even home—the sanctuary they returned to after the job. Office time meant kicking back, catching up with friends, sparring with superiors, and, heck, flirting with some of the folk in other divisions. Outside, they had to be alert and ready for anything, but at HQ, they could switch off and relax. It was the opposite of normal employment, but it made their attachment to the Shinra Building all the more heartfelt.

So they reacted badly when the building was hit, and it got even worse when they learned that Rufus, the company president, was nowhere to be found.

Many witnesses had seen the president's office take a direct hit from one Weapon's energy beam. This meant that the odds of the president still being alive were remote at best.

It wasn't just the president, either. The status of a good deal of upper management, including all the executive directors, could not be confirmed. The company's chain of command was in utter disarray. With Meteor about to strike the planet in a matter of days, most employees had simply deserted their posts.

Reno and Rude's first job was to find out if Rufus was still alive, but getting to the executive levels proved tricky. The secure express elevators that went directly to the top floors weren't running, and so they were forced to head up in stages via the slower, short-distance elevators used by ordinary employees.

"Man, this one isn't running, either," Reno complained.

"Maybe they all went into emergency shutdown," said Rude.

"Oh yeah, 'cause *that's* helpful in an emergency."

"You two. Stop bickering and take the stairs."

The two exchanged a glance and then turned. Behind them stood a familiar figure with long black hair—the last person they had expected to see here. "Chief!"

Days ago, they had been told that Tseng was KIA. The rookie, Elena, had sworn to avenge him and had taken off for the far north in pursuit of Cloud, only to fail and return to Midgar cursing Cloud's name. Reno and Rude could practically still hear her muttering, "I'll make him pay! I will!" under her breath like an incantation. As far as any of them had known, Tseng really was dead.

"What are you staring at? And close your mouths," said Tseng.

"You're...*alive*?" Rude managed.

"Obviously. But there's no time for a debriefing."

"Right." Reno nodded vigorously, letting his boss know he'd already taken everything in his stride.

"Tseng!" It was the voice of a young woman. The three turned together to see Elena, the rookie, making no attempt to contain her joy at seeing her commander back from the dead. She ran straight up to Tseng and threw her arms around him.

"Look, Elena," said Reno, "we're all happy to see the chief, but—"

"But what? I know you want to hug him, too," she said.

"I think I'll pass."

After Tseng managed to extricate himself from Elena's embrace, he looked resolutely at his three operatives and nodded. "Let's get to work."

Darkness, and more darkness. The monstrous Weapon had struck the building. Now, Rufus Shinra was sliding down a never-ending slope, laughing all the way.

It seemed unimaginable that such a beast could exist on the planet. But exist it did, and when it fired at the Shinra Building, hitting close to the president's office, the shock wave had thrown Rufus to the floor. Other explosions followed, the ceiling collapsed, and a steel beam crashed down mere inches from his head. There would be more falling debris where that came from. He rolled under the desk, hoping it would provide some protection.

When he saw the fire from the monster heading straight for the building, he had been prepared to die. But after the shock wave only knocked him down, anger replaced resignation. Rufus was furious with himself for accepting death so readily, without protest. *What was I thinking? I shouldn't be welcoming death; I should be laughing in its face!*

The anger gave him focus. The Weapon might fire again. He had to get out, and fast.

From his refuge under the desk, Rufus scanned the room looking for exits. What caught his eye was a small switch marked *L*.

It was on the underside of the desk, designed to be concealed. Something hidden *here* could only be something for emergencies—such as the one in which he found himself. He flipped the switch without a moment's hesitation.

The section of floor beneath his back disappeared with a *clunk*. Helplessly, he fell a few feet and landed on his back on a hard surface.

The surface was tilted. He began to slide, faster and faster.

Okay. So instead of dying in the explosion, I'm going to fall to my death in an air duct.

His predicament struck him as ridiculous. What would people think when they found his body, stuck upside down in a duct, halfway down the building? Or jammed in a ventilation fan? While the world was locked in a desperate battle for the fate of the planet itself, the president of Shinra, the organization that was supposed to save them, was falling to his death through a hole in his own office.

He'd laugh, if it weren't for his impending death.

And who built this duct anyway? Why was it at an angle, like a slide? Why was that switch labeled with an *L*?

Then Rufus remembered a conversation with his father from almost twenty years ago. And then he did laugh.

Five-year-old Rufus woke up in the middle of the night and noticed that, for once, his father was home. He went into the room prepared for no more than a gruff "Go to bed!"

But the old man was in unusually high spirits. He showed Rufus some blueprints. Fresh from the architects, he said—they were plans for the upcoming renovation of the president's office in the Shinra Building. "What do you think? I'll be running the entire world from there."

"Wow." Rufus pretended to be impressed while he stared hard at the plans, trying to glean something from them. Something that would earn him praise for being clever. But, unable to find anything, he instead asked a question. "Father, how do you escape?"

The old man creased his forehead.

"What do you mean, *escape?*"

"If somebody attacks, how do you get out?"

"Listen, boy. The Shinra Company has no enemies who'd dare attack me. And even if they did, the president's office is seventy floors up. No way could an attacker get up that far. Not with the security we have in place."

"Mr. Palmer said there could be attacks from space."

"Did he, now?" The creases in the old man's brow deepened. That meant he was angry.

Palmer was the director of the company's space program, and it sounded like he might be in trouble later. But Palmer always said it was his job to get yelled at, so Rufus wasn't worried for him. *As long as the old man doesn't yell at* me, Rufus thought. But he could tell he'd ruined his father's good mood. "Sorry, Father. I'm getting sleepy."

"Tell you what, Rufus." President Shinra ignored his son's attempt to extricate himself. "If you're that worried, I'll get them to add an escape route in case of an attack. Not for me, mind. But it'll be there for you when you become president. Assuming you work hard and prove you've got what it takes. No guarantees, remember?"

"Father—"

"Hmph. As if I'd ever need to *escape*."

"I'm sorry, Father."

"What are you apologizing for? Are you admitting that your idea was wrong?"

"Maybe it was."

"Ha! At least you're honest about it."

By this point, Rufus could think only of getting away.

"I'll make sure to label it so it's easy to find for someone who wants to *escape*. It'll be marked *L*. Got that? *L* for *Loser*."

Rufus wished he could go back and shake the hand of his five-year-old self.

He seemed to have been sliding down the escape chute forever. It must go all the way down to the lowest levels. Rufus found himself with plenty of time to reflect on his life. Trivial incidents he'd all but forgotten came back to him, and when he realized his father featured in most of them, it struck him that he had always been seeking his father's approval, trying desperately to surpass the old man. But he'd gone about it all the wrong way, with petty acts of rebellion and disloyalty that incurred his father's wrath rather than his respect.

The banality of it all struck him as funny. Here he was, a grown man going down a slide in the dark, brooding as he went about childhood slights and a father's disapproval.

Finally, the chute ended, and Rufus was hurled at high speed into a small white room, brightly lit. He let out a grunt as he slammed into the opposite wall.

"Eep!"

Had that pathetic sound come from himself? Ridiculous. It felt like he had broken some ribs, but he still couldn't stop laughing at himself, crumpled upside down in a heap against the wall like a discarded puppet. Eventually, though, the bout of near-hysteria passed, and the pain of the broken bones forced him back into the present.

Still lying on the floor, he struggled into a position that hurt less and looked around the room to take stock of the situation. The room was about sixteen feet square. Next to the chute from which he'd emerged, there was a simple cot, dressed with clean linen sheets that nonetheless had a fine layer of dust over them. The entirety of the wall to the right was taken up by a closet. To the left, there was a steel door.

Bracing himself against the pain, Rufus dragged himself over to the door and examined it from where he lay on the floor. He saw no doorknob or handle of any kind, but there was a small input panel, which likely controlled the door. Perhaps there was an access code. But he had no idea what it might be, not even how many digits it would be, and right now he didn't have the energy to figure it out. So he ignored the door and went to the closet on the opposite side, pushing himself across the floor with his legs as he lay on his back. He was glad no one was around to see this.

At least the closet was easy to open. It was packed with sealed boxes printed with the Shinra logo. He took one from the lowest shelf, since he couldn't reach any higher, and found that the lid was marked To: L.

Rufus snorted. And then once again laughter rose uncontrollably from his gut, but the stabbing pain from his ribs quelled it as quickly as it came.

He opened the box. Inside were potions and various bottles and packages containing conventional medicine. Magical potions could degrade and turn poisonous over time, so he set those aside, tossed back a synthetic painkiller, and waited for the effect to kick in. As he lay there, he looked at the ceiling. It was emblazoned with a giant *L*.

"Don't make me laugh any more, old man."

He took more of the painkiller than he should have, and the hours drifted by in a haze. The power of modern medicine made it comfortable here in the shelter, but it didn't entirely numb the frustration of being removed from the action. At a time like this, he needed to be out there. Organizing a response. Providing leadership.

At length, he pulled himself to his feet, leaned against the wall by the control panel, and tried entering different codes. No good. His concentration faltered; he didn't have the energy to focus on the problem. It was the drug's fault, he knew. Still, he gulped down more of it anyway.

Reno and Rude stood in the wreckage of the president's office.

"Not a trace."

"Yep."

"We checked three times, right?"

"Thoroughly."

"So maybe he's alive."

"Could be."

Several steel beams had fallen from the ceiling and smashed into the floor of the office. They had been careful to search under them to make sure Rufus had not been trapped there.

"But where do we start looking?"

As Meteor drew closer, it had begun to affect the atmosphere and kick up gale-force winds. The Turks ignored the storms and the threat looming in the sky as they continued to search for Rufus. They had directed rescue workers to scour the building, but as yet there was still no sign of the president.

Reno and Rude decided to search an area at the back of the first-floor main entrance of the building. An inconspicuous door led to a series of sublevel passageways that in normal times were reserved for executive use only. President Shinra, the previous head of the company, had supervised the construction of the zone, and the interior reflected his tastes. Apart from the stately entrance, there was little by way of decoration. The ceilings, the walls, the floors—everything was covered in unadorned steel plates.

"There's nothing here," said Reno. "C'mon, Rude. We're wastin' our time."

"Wait." Rude held up a hand and pointed to a section of the wall. "Is it just me, or is that wall section a different color?"

Rufus was propped against the wall, staring at the panel and the keys numbered 0 through 9. It crossed his mind that he *could* try all the possible numeric combinations. Which would get him out of here, he calculated, at some point within forty thousand years or so. *Scratch that option off the list*, he thought.

Unless his father had chosen a truly random code—in which case, that forty-thousand-year option was all he had—he *could* work it out. It might be a sequence of numbers that stood for something, but whatever it was, it didn't help if it only meant something to his father and not him. So far, the few numbers he had tried that might have some significance to them both—like his mother's birthday, and the day she had died—failed to unlock the door.

He didn't know how much time had passed since his rough landing in the room. But the fact that he was still alive meant Meteor hadn't yet struck. It was only a matter of time, of course. The Sister Ray had failed to work, Sephiroth was still in his crater, and there was nothing left that could stop Meteor from striking the planet.

Rufus thought about his death. Supposedly, human spirits merged into the Lifestream that coursed through the earth. He imagined meeting the spirit of his father and talking to him, though it was hard to picture. What sort of form did a disembodied spirit take? But of course, he knew it didn't work like that anyway. The consciousness of individuals probably could not survive long in the overwhelming torrent of the planet's energy.

But then he remembered that the planet itself was unlikely to survive the coming cataclysm. So none of them could even look forward to an afterlife floating in the Lifestream. The hopelessness of it all made him laugh again.

He reached into the pocket of his white suit for the bottle of painkillers. He tossed three tablets into his mouth and stared at the panel as he chewed.

I know I'm dead anyway, he thought, *but I'd rather not die in here.*

There was one sequence of numbers he hadn't yet tried, though it had been on his mind since he first saw the control panel. It felt like pinning his hopes on *that* number would be to admit that the old man got another one over him, again. But then, did that matter anymore?

Reno and Rude examined the steel paneling. As Rude had said, it was a different color than the surrounding panels, but that was the only thing that set it apart.

"It was probably just a replacement panel or something. C'mon, let's get outta—"

Reno stopped midsentence. The three-foot-wide panel was sliding downward, disappearing into a slot at the base of the wall.

They looked at each other and then peered through the hole. Beyond, they could see a small white room.

"Uh, hello?" Reno was about to step in when Rufus emerged from behind the wall.

"Ah, just who I needed to see," said the young leader of Shinra, before he collapsed to the ground.

"Boss!"

As Reno held Rufus, Rude poked his head into the white room.

He gave the place a once-over. It was clearly a panic room or emergency shelter. Next to the door, there was a control panel, where four digits blinked on the display. There was no way for Rude to know it, but the code number was the same number the previous president had used for all his devices. It was a series of numbers he would never have forgotten—his son's birthday.

"Hey, Rude, call in medical already!" Reno shouted. "And how about a sitrep on what's going on outside?"

"How is he?" said Rude.

"Tired. Injured. Fast asleep. But alive."

The president's breathing was deep and even.

"Guess he figured he could relax, once he saw the cavalry had shown up." But his attempt at levity felt hollow.

"Good," Rude replied, then headed outside. He meant it, too.

In the darkness of the storm-racked night, Rude stood at the back exit of the Shinra Building. The ground was littered with panels of the facade, twisted metal, and chunks of concrete that had fallen from the building. Shards of broken glass glittered in the floodlights that had been deployed to assist the efforts of the rescue workers. Above them, helicopters swept the scene with searchlights.

Rude found himself taking it all in with a measure of calm. The fact that Rufus was alive had restored his confidence. Rufus *was* the Shinra Company. For better or worse, Shinra was still operational, more or less. And as long as Shinra existed, so would the Turks.

It was too painful to think of a life without the Turks.

A fist-size chunk of wood, caught in the powerful downdraft of a low-flying chopper, flew inches past his head at injurious speed. Rude smiled. He loved danger, and danger loved him. With Rufus back from the dead, Rude knew there'd be more dangerous work ahead for him.

He made his way around the building, stepping over the scattered debris as he went. Terrified people were crouched down here and there, cowering from the winds and perhaps also from the sight of arms and legs protruding from under the wreckage.

Rude checked the people who had been trapped, looking for survivors. Those who were alive would sometimes recoil in fear when they saw him. With his clean-shaven head and gleaming shades, he exuded menace. He was used to their reaction. It gave him grim satisfaction, to see he still earned it even in a crisis.

Some of the rescue workers scurrying around were staff from a company-funded hospital. Rude grabbed one of them and told him there was an injured man inside the building who needed attention. He carefully omitted the name Rufus. He didn't want to cause a stir.

"A Shinra employee?" asked the doctor.

"That's right."

"We'll make it a top priority."

"Good."

The doctor nodded and called to a colleague who had a stretcher, and they hurried around to the back of the building. As he watched them go, Rude thought he'd better go after them and make sure they were able to find Rufus. As he did so, he caught sight of a young girl talking on a phone.

It was one of Cloud's pals, a girl named Yuffie. She was considered hostile to the Shinra Company and on the Turks' Persons of Interest list. But there was no need to engage now. Fighting was something he did only when directed or when someone tried to interfere with an operation.

Rude watched as she scampered off, her light-footed figure darting through the shadows and over the debris.

"Where will you take him?" Reno said, helping the rescue worker get Rufus onto the stretcher.

"To the hospital for now. But after that, who knows?"

"What do you mean?"

"I mean, have you happened to notice that big rock in the sky? When that thing hits, all bets are off. We're going to keep trying to help people, but frankly, there doesn't seem much point."

"Fair enough. C'mon, this way." Reno led the rescue worker through a small door out to the main lobby.

"Huh. Didn't know that door was there. The bald guy could've told us there was a shortcut."

"Executive use only. So don't go tellin' your friends."

"Yes, sir. I can keep my mouth shut."

Satisfied with the reply, Reno nodded and continued on toward the exit. He was almost out of the building when he spotted the back of Yuffie's head disappearing around a corner.

"You got this? I just saw someone who might be a problem," he asked the worker.

"Of course, sir. We'll handle it. Who is this patient, by the way?"

"He'll tell you himself when he wakes up. Just make sure you put him in the best room you've got. All the bells and whistles."

"Boss? Th-this guy looks a lot like Rufus Shinra," whispered one of the men carrying the stretcher.

"Shh!"

Later, people would come to call it "the chosen day" or, more simply and ominously, "that day." Rufus was in the town of Kalm, a short distance from Midgar, when the astounding event occurred.

The hospital was in chaos, overrun with patients, and it would have been impossible to ensure the president's safety there. When Rufus had regained consciousness, the Turks charged with his protection convinced him to move to a modest company-owned residence in Kalm. They could have used the helicopter to take him farther from the city, but Rufus said no. He had only agreed to move out of Midgar with reluctance, and he would not run any farther than Kalm. When the world teetered on the verge of annihilation, trying to run and hide just looked bad.

Four Turks moved through the doomed city of Midgar. Meteor was so close, it seemed they could reach up and touch it. They had already carried out their main duty and gotten Rufus to safety—although safety was a relative concept at best, with an apocalypse looming. But end of the world or not, they still had jobs to do, and they would not give up on them while they still lived.

"There's no point in dwelling on what will happen when Meteor hits. We have to operate under the assumption that the worst will be averted," Tseng had announced when he issued orders for the Turks to organize the evacuation of Midgar.

The city was already feeling the effects of Meteor's proximity. Windstorms were growing more ferocious, and earthquakes shook the slums and Plate zones alike, bringing down buildings and infrastructure. In the throes of Nature's fury, the metal city creaked and groaned.

"So now at the end of the world we're supposed to become do-gooders. Figures, considering who's giving out the orders," said Rude, half under his breath.

"How so?" said Reno.

"Chief is trying to clear his conscience, is how so."

"Oh. Yeah, that makes sense."

When Reno saw their former commander Verdot in Midgar with some of their old comrades, he wondered if Meteor was making him hallucinate.

Once in the past, the Turks had acted against the company's interests. They had done it only to save the world. Saving Verdot and his daughter in the process was incidental. Still, what they'd done was against the rules. When he looked back at it, Reno thought that time might have been a high point for camaraderie in the Turks, and that the Turks would never feel like that again. But as they came together to help out the shocked and bedraggled citizens of Midgar, it started to feel like those days once more. He was enjoying this last kick at the can.

In the wake of that incident, President Shinra and the other execs had decided to disband the Turks and terminate the organization—with extreme prejudice. The one who saved both their lives and their jobs had been the then–vice president, one Rufus Shinra. The Turks had been in his debt ever since.

They'd paid part of that debt in the last few days, when they rescued Rufus and got him to the relative safety of Kalm. Now Reno was working side by side with friends and colleagues he'd never expected to meet again. Even if they had only a few days left, he thought, he wouldn't end up with too many regrets.

*   *

Meteor was shattered in the sky above Midgar, and the planet was saved from destruction, thanks to the Lifestream that burst out of the ground. It was the triumph of the ultimate white magic, Holy, over the ultimate black magic of Meteor. The battle waged by Cloud and his friends was essential to the victory, but people could only know what they saw, and they believed that it was the planet itself that had saved them from annihilation.

Reno and Rude were in the Shinra Building when it happened, directly below Meteor.

"Oh man. *Now* what?" said Reno as the Lifestream cascaded in a furious rush around the building, causing it to shudder and sway. It poured in through the windows and smashed everything in its path like an unstoppable rush of water breaching a dam. Reno and Rude scampered to the safest place they could find, which happened to be the restroom stalls.

"This is my fault," said Rude through the wall. They were each in their own stall.

"What is?"

"Us being here. I wanted to get my kit, and now…," he muttered. Reno realized he was apologizing, sort of.

"It's cool. Don't beat yourself up over it."

Wasn't like Reno to cut anyone slack like that. Rude didn't know what to say.

"Rude?" Reno couldn't stand the silence, apparently.

"What?"

"Y'know, we've been working together for a pretty long time."

"Guess so."

"Like partners. Are we partners?"

"Sure."

"Heeey, partner."

That sounded like the usual Reno, for whatever reason. Rude heard Reno leaving his stall. *What's he up to?*

He soon had his answer. Reno suddenly kicked in the door of Rude's stall. Rude blocked the flying door just in time and kicked it back.

"What the hell?!"

"Just one last present for my partner."

"A bathroom door?"

"A thrill! Your favorite."

"I've had better thrills eating breakfast," Rude retorted, stepping out of the busted stall.

"Enough messing around. How about we go outside? I bet it's insane out there."

"I'm sure it is."

*　　*　　*

The two Turks stepped out of the Shinra Building's main entrance and into a howling tempest. Writhing tendrils of light were streaming out of the ground into the air, right in front of their eyes.

"Holy shit! The Lifestream's *everywhere*, man!"

"Reno..."

"Yeah?"

"This is awesome."

*　　　　*

"Tseng, Reno, Rude, Elena..." The morning after the Lifestream tore through Midgar, Rufus addressed the four of them. "What are your plans?"

"Uh, I don't remember getting a pink slip," said Reno.

The other three nodded, clearly on the same page.

So Rufus gave the Turks two orders: Go back to Midgar to evaluate the situation and gather allies.

"Keep in mind, not everyone affiliated with the company is going to be friendly now," he told them.

"Got it. But what do we need allies for?"

"Information, for now. As much as we can get." With multiple broken ribs and a fractured foot, not to mention serious bruising, Rufus was for the time being confined to a wheelchair. His air of cool authority, however, was unchanged.

"Tseng?"

"Sir."

"I thought you might be ready to retire."

"Not at all, sir. There's much to be done that only Shinra can accomplish," Tseng replied evenly.

Rufus looked pleased.

"Well. If nothing else, you won't be bored."

After a short break for sleep and food, the Turks headed back into Midgar and split into two groups. Tseng and Elena set out to gather intelligence, while Reno and Rude searched for allies. Other Turk comrades who had been here yesterday were already gone, scattering across the planet and working to relay intelligence to Kalm from places far beyond Midgar.

"Avalanche used to say Shinra was the enemy of the planet," Reno recalled.

"Uh-huh."

"Guess they were kinda right."

"How so?" said Rude.

"I mean, *look*."

Reno gestured vaguely at the whole city. The Lifestream had saved the planet from Meteor, but in the process, it had wrought terrible damage on Midgar. In many ways, the city had been like a castle town of olden times, one that had sprung up to serve the ruling lords in the towering fortress that was the Shinra Building. If the city wasn't entirely flattened, it looked beyond repair. It was not quite a death sentence, but at the same time, it was hard to imagine it returning to life.

As people came to understand that the company had failed to save them from the disaster, they would turn against Shinra. They would need someone to blame, and the company's name was right there, emblazoned on everything.

Reno and Rude made it to Sector Zero but not to the Shinra Building. The damage was especially bad here. What actually blocked their way, however, were the crowds of people clamoring for information and aid.

"Oh, *that's* rich," Reno spit, catching some conversations. People were calling Shinra the root of all evil and in the next breath declaring that the company had to fix everything.

"I'm starting to get the urge to knock heads together."

"Go for it," said Rude. "I won't stop you."

"Nah. Gotta think about the company image, right?"

Tseng and Elena headed below the Plate to Wall Market in the Sector Six slum, an area the Turks had always found to be a rich source of intel—though not all of it the best quality. Debris falling from the structure above had caused heavy damage throughout the neighborhood, but the place didn't look all that different for it. This was the slums, after all.

The biggest difference was in the population, which had shrunk dramatically. Rumors were spreading that the entire city of Midgar was on the verge of collapse, and the timid and not-so-timid alike were fleeing the looming shadow of the Plate.

As they explored, Tseng and Elena were also hearing people express less than stellar reviews of Shinra. Some even threw rocks—from a safe distance—when they recognized the distinctive suits of the Turks.

"This is going to make it hard to do our job," said Elena. "Maybe we should change into something less conspicuous."

They picked up new outfits at the first store they found. Tseng ended up in a loud floral shirt of the type that vacationers always wore back from Costa del Sol, while Elena slipped into something sleek and trendy. Suitably disguised, they hit a bar that still had a decent-size clientele. Most of the tables were full, but they found seats in a corner and took in their surroundings. A lone man in a black shirt, occupying a table meant for four, caught Tseng's attention.

"It looks like he's passed out," said Elena.

"I wonder..."

"Tseng?"

"Yes?"

"The reason I stayed with the Turks is—I mean, apart from pride and duty, because that's really important and everything—but, actually, the main reason personally is, erm..."

Elena's feelings for her commander had never exactly been a secret, but that didn't make it any easier to tell him, out loud, in so many words. She paused, tongue-tied.

"Good. Keep yapping," Tseng urged.

"Huh?"

"We're trying to blend in. It doesn't look natural if we sit here in stone silence. Drivel like that is perfect. Just keep moving your mouth."

"Sure, right... Er, drivel." She sighed sadly, but he wasn't looking at her. He was still staring at the unconscious man.

"Something's wrong." Tseng got up and went to the man with his face on the table.

"Are you all right?"

There was no answer. Tseng grabbed the man's shoulder, meaning to give him a shake, but his hand met something gooey. He jerked away and found some kind of viscous black stuff on his palm.

He looked more carefully. He hadn't noticed before because of the black shirt, but the man's torso was soaked in dark slime.

"What's the matter with him?" Elena asked, coming over to see.

"He's dead."

Reno and Rude had finally reached the main lobby of the Shinra Building. Reno was writing a message on a large notice board that stood there:

Anyone who wants to get off the Plate, take the train tracks down to the slums. The trains aren't running. There are no plans to restore service. You'll have to walk. There are no supplies here. Shinra Electric Power Company operations are indefinitely suspended.

The two-story house in Kalm had a living and dining room on the first floor, useful for meetings, as well as a small kitchen and a bath unit. The second floor had three bedrooms, and Rufus had settled in one of these. With his foot in a cast and his torso bound in braces to protect his ribs, he still needed a wheelchair to get around most of the time.

The window afforded a view of the town. Through a small gap between the drawn curtains, he could see the streets packed with people. The Lifestream had caused damage in Kalm, too, but buildings were intact and the homes still habitable, and refugees streaming in from Midgar were stopping here in search of shelter.

Rufus was surprised by their sheer numbers. As far back as he could remember, he had never been around such a mass of people without security or an escort of some kind. Only a single wall separated him from all the fear and desperation outside, and that stark reality did his nerves no favors. It wasn't even a sturdy reinforced wall like those of the Shinra Building—just thin wood and plaster. A strong man could punch his way through.

Tseng had offered to assign a security detail, and he had refused. Now he smiled wryly at his pointless pride.

He considered his situation. The Shinra Building was a fortress built by his old man. That made it, more or less, a symbol of his father. For a son to become his own man, he had to venture out from under his father's roof and make his own way, survive by his own hand. It was how things were. Now, that day had come for him. He did not need to cower from the public. He was ready to leap into the fray and do what he was meant to do—which, he believed, was to rebuild the world.

The doorbell rang. A few moments passed before it rang a second time. Rufus ignored it, but it kept ringing, twice more, three times.

This wasn't the sequence they had discussed. The caller wasn't anyone he knew.

Then he heard the sound of someone trying to kick open the door. Perhaps it was just a desperate refugee. Rufus wheeled himself to the bed and took the pistol from under his pillow. He hid the gun in the folds of his hospital gown, turned the chair by the window toward the bedroom door, and then laboriously moved himself into it from the wheelchair.

Rufus had reinforced the front door, and whoever was trying to break it down appeared to give up. Then Rufus heard the sound of a breaking window, followed by footsteps inside the house. More than one person.

"Not what I needed today." He flicked off the safety.

In the twilight, Elena and Tseng were headed back to Kalm, discussing the sickness they'd seen in the slums. When they talked to the locals, they learned that a good number of others were showing the same symptoms as the dead man in the bar.

"What *happened* while I was out of commission?" said Tseng.

"I've not seen it before, either. Whatever it is, it appeared fast," said Elena.

Tseng wondered if the sickness, or poison, or whatever it was, had only started ravaging Midgar today. Otherwise, they surely would have known about it already. Was it too much of a coincidence that the Lifestream had erupted the day before the illness appeared? Had the Lifestream affected people as well as wrecking the city?

"I just hope this doesn't spark a full-blown panic," he remarked.

"I think it's too late." Elena was talking about the scene they'd witnessed when the other patrons noticed that someone had died there in the bar. First, they crowded closer with morbid curiosity, and then they broke out into a panic, scrambling for the exit when someone shouted that it could be contagious.

Reno and Rude made it back to Kalm first. They would have liked to take a chopper or at least a car, but no one knew how much longer the fuel would last. For now, at least, it was being strictly rationed.

"Let's try Sector Five tomorrow," said Rude.

"Company housing? Doubt we'll find anything new. Unless you think Shinra people are still hunkered down there."

"I'm talking about the warehouses. We could get supplies. Vehicles, ammo, heavy weapons."

"Weapons. Good point. I've got a feeling we'll be needing plenty of them."

Thinking of Midgar's miserable survivors and the resentment that must be simmering in them, Reno heaved a sigh.

*   *   *

The men stood surrounding Rufus.

"Looks like you've been knocked around pretty badly, *Mr. President*." A bearded man who carried himself like the leader jabbed a shotgun at Rufus.

"Indeed I have. Though I'm more worried now than I was then. There's nothing quite as dangerous as men with grievances and a fool leading them." He stared straight into the man's bloodshot eyes.

He expected they would force him to hear a litany of complaints before killing him. Even if he could take down one or two of them with the gun concealed in his sleeve, he could hear a small mob downstairs in addition to the three here in the bedroom. They'd overpower him eventually.

"Call me a fool if ya want, but we all know who's got to answer for what happened."

"Oh? Then tell me this. What are you going to do after you walk out of here? Have you thought about what's coming?"

"What're you talking about?"

"There are two kinds of people—those who command and those who obey," said Rufus. "It's not a question of innate qualities or earned merit. Often enough, when things go wrong, the people in command are punished for it. Then the people left behind have no one to follow. Chaos naturally ensues. And instead of things improving, everything gets even worse."

"If you're trying to convince me to spare yer life, it ain't workin'," said the man with a sneer.

"You seem to be in command of this mob that broke in here. So what's your endgame? What kind of future can you promise them?"

"Screw the future. It's enough for us if we make it to the end of the day. Tomorrow can sort itself out."

"Do all of you think that way? Or is it just you?" Rufus noticed the other two men starting to glance between him and their leader.

"So, what? You think we should be doing something different?" one of them asked.

Rufus looked him over. Midthirties, fit. Dressed in an expensive-looking navy jacket, albeit torn and covered in dust.

"Of course," he replied. "First of all, someone needs to find a place for the refugees. Kalm can't possibly accommodate all the people fleeing Midgar. I'm guessing you're from this town."

"That's right."

"Do you want it to turn into another Midgar?"

"…"

Rufus could see the man working out what would happen if all the refugees ended up staying where they were.

"We're not going to turn people away!" The man with the shotgun was done being ignored.

"Fine. What about when the weather turns bad? What are those people down in the streets going to do? Yes, this is a time of crisis. It's right to offer hospitality. But you have to think long-term. How many people live in Midgar? There's no room here for them all. Are you prepared to deal with their need to be fed, to be clothed, to be housed? Can you tell *them* it's good enough to make it to the end of the day?"

"Shut up! You talk too much!" The leader was shouting now, acting just as Rufus calculated. He knew his type. A sergeant. Good at leading a small platoon…but not a larger group of people. Never an army.

"All right. You made your point. So what's your plan, Mr. Shinra?" the man in the navy jacket said. His voice carried well. *This one might be the true leader among the bunch*, Rufus thought.

"If I told you, you'd have much less reason to keep me alive."

When they got back into town, Reno and Rude found a very different scene from the one they'd left in the morning.

"This is a lot of people."

Even on the street that took them "home," it was more of the same. In fact, it was immediately apparent that strangers had paid a visit to said home.

"Boss!"

They dashed up to the house. The door was standing open, but when they looked in, they saw that the entranceway was blocked by men and women huddled on the floor, some of them stretched out and unconscious.

"They're sick," said Rude.

They could see a dark fluid staining clothes and bandages—it was the same affliction they'd seen in Midgar. It appeared that the house had been turned into a makeshift hospital.

"Rude, you check down here." Reno picked his way among the sick people, trying not to step on anyone, and sprinted up the stairs. A similar sight greeted him at the top. Worried now, he went through the rooms looking for Rufus but found no sign of him. He went back down to Rude.

"I don't see him," Rude reported.

"Me neither. We should get out of here, pronto. I don't want to catch whatever these people have got."

One of the patients glared at him angrily, and Reno returned the stare with what he hoped was a winning grin. It wasn't like he meant to be mean or anything.

Rude shoved him outside, and there they ran into Tseng and Elena, who were just arriving.

"Tseng, the house's been taken over." Reno briefly apprised their commander of the situation.

"Our priority is to find the president," Tseng said. "He might have been kidnapped. Someone here must know what happened."

"I'll ask inside. Don't want you guys scaring everyone into silence." Elena headed for the house.

"Elena, they're sick," said Reno. "Be careful in there."

"If it *is* contagious, it's too late to be worrying about it now."

Well, she's right about that, Reno realized. The four of them might have all gotten it already.

"Now, you two." Tseng gave a single order to Reno and Rude. "Go into town and find witnesses."

The pair nodded silently and set off in separate directions.

After some time, the three Turks reported back to Tseng, their faces drawn and weary. They had found no witnesses. People were angry with Shinra, and they weren't shy about letting them know it.

"Not surprising. These people have got their hands full dealing with their own problems," Tseng said quietly, watching a man being carried down the street, too ill or badly hurt to walk. "And besides…"

But he trailed off, leaving the thought unsaid. *There might well be witnesses*, he thought. *Just none willing to talk to the Turks.*

Rufus estimated that about two weeks had passed since he'd been taken from the house in Kalm. They had grabbed his gun, then held to his face a handkerchief reeking of some kind of drug. He'd fallen unconscious and awoken in another house. Where, he had no idea. One of the men had let slip it was a villa belonging to the man in the navy jacket. Mütten, he called himself, though Rufus had doubts as to whether that was his real name.

Rufus guessed he was being kept in the basement. He could hear people walking around above him. If they were refugees, then he might still be in Kalm, rather than somewhere more remote. On the other hand, they could just be more members of Mütten's gang.

With no conclusions to be reached on his own, he had little choice but to wait things out in his prison until the Turks found him. *And a strange prison it is*, thought Rufus. The decor was nearly entirely crimson—luxurious but hinting at unsavory tastes, thanks to the furnishings carved with disturbing images of human-monster chimeras. There were fetters around his ankles. They were attached by a heavy chain to a sturdy iron hook on the wall. The idea that someone, perhaps Mütten, had clearly set this up as a prison beforehand gave Rufus an unpleasant chill. With his injuries, he didn't exactly need to be chained up in the first place. The excessive measures did not bode well.

Apart from denying him his freedom, however, Mütten was otherwise treating Rufus well. A middle-aged woman, probably a housekeeper, saw to his meals and his comfort as best she could. Rufus tried to ask her questions, but she refused to speak to him; she had probably been ordered not to.

A doctor who looked to be in his fifties came to see him once. After a perfunctory checkup, he left Rufus with some medicine. If he knew the patient chained up in this strange basement room was the president of the Shinra Company, he gave no indication of it. Rufus thought of shouting for help to the people upstairs as they came and went, but he feared that might only make things worse for him.

Once every few days, Mütten made an appearance, asking Rufus about his plan to develop an area near Midgar. Rufus had intended to flesh out the plan after the Turks had brought him more information, but of course his present situation made that impossible. Lacking the data he needed, Rufus could only sketch out the bare bones of his idea: First, establish a new town adjacent to Midgar. The east side, where the terrain was flattest, would be the best location and make construction easier. Materials could be salvaged from the wreckage in Midgar. The company had cutting torches and welding supplies, as well as small-scale construction equipment, in the Sector Five storehouses.

He only revealed the plan in small pieces. He feared that once Mütten had everything he needed from him, he would be killed. He felt like the storyteller in that fairy tale, who would be killed unless she came up with a new tale, night after night, to entertain the king. Rufus laughed wryly at the thought.

"Why don't you just tell me everything? I'm not going to kill you."

"Why don't you undo my chains? I'm not going to run away."

It seemed they would never reach a point of mutual trust.

The Turks had found tantalizing leads, scraps of information, but nothing that turned into anything concrete when they looked into it. They were no closer to finding their missing president than when they had started.

Tseng was not about to give up the search, however. They left the house in Kalm to the squatting refugees and set up base in a company house in Sector Five. At Elena's suggestion, they deliberately disseminated the rumor that Midgar was on the verge of collapse. Many of those who still remained in Midgar believed it and left. But while that part might be disinformation, the city was in fact barely habitable. It had become a wretched place strewn with rubble and rife with disease, and before much longer, it would be completely deserted. The Turks preferred that it would happen sooner rather than later. There were too many company secrets hidden here, and they especially wanted to keep the Shinra arsenal from falling into the hands of the public.

"So, uh, this is bad." It was Reno who brought the news. "Some military forces that were based in Junon have come up here and taken over the HQ. About a hundred troops, they reckon. The guy in command is one Lieutenant...er, Something-gate."

"What do they want?" said Tseng.

"Dunno. But it looks like they're gearing up for something."

Tseng and Elena went to check out the situation at the Shinra Building, while Reno and Rude set out to collect ammo and weapons.

The company houses were densely packed into one corner of Sector Five, while the storehouses were located in the restricted area near the mako reactor. High fences ran around the perimeter, and there was only one point of access—a secure gate that was impossible to open without an access code. In an emergency, the code automatically switched to one that was known only to those with certain high-level clearance. Still reciting over in their heads the code that Tseng had given them, Reno and Rude arrived at the gate...to find it standing wide-open.

"Think those military guys have been here?"

"Could be."

Alert now, they went in and moved toward Building Eight, where most of the munitions were stored. Halfway there, though, they noticed that the service entrance to Building Four was standing open. Staying in the shadows, Reno and Rude crept inside.

"Huh? Civilians," said Reno.

Bands of young men and women, even children, were moving around inside the building.

"Building Four is construction equipment," said Rude.

Indeed, they could see that the civilians were pulling small and medium-size machinery off the shelves. Even the children were pitching in, carrying tools and drills and the like.

"What's going on?" muttered Reno, and just then they heard cheers from outside, in front of the next-door building. People must have managed to open that door, too.

"Shit. Building Five. That would be the fuel reserves."

"What, like mako?"

"No, fossil fuels. Gas and diesel mostly. Shinra stored it there for emergencies. We're gonna need it, too."

"Ugh. One thing after another."

Reno didn't want trouble, and he certainly didn't want to start a firefight with civs. He tried to keep from sounding too threatening as he approached the people outside Building Five.

"So, hey. We're with the Shinra Company. Is anyone in charge here?"

"I am." A good-looking woman stepped forward. She was young. Still a girl, really.

"You're in charge of all this?" Reno blinked in surprise.

"So what are you people up to?" said Rude, his voice much lower than Reno's. An uneasy look crossed the girl's face.

"We're just taking some equipment. We need it to build a new place for—"

"On whose authority?"

"Officer Kylegate. With the military."

"Did this Kylegate give you the access codes, too?"

"Yes. Um, is there a problem? We were given permission to be here. We heard that the Shinra military was going to start reconstruction operations, independent of the company. They asked for volunteers, so we stepped up."

She glanced nervously from one to the other of them. Reno and Rude exchanged a look. Maybe the military had some hidden agenda, but if they did, this girl and the other civilians clearly weren't in on it.

"If that's really what you're doing, then we've got no problem," Reno said, after getting a small nod from Rude.

"But do us a favor. Don't take any more than you need from the fuel reserves. Live frugally," added Rude.

"Sure, no prob." She looked relieved as she turned back to her work.

Reno and Rude watched as the volunteers gathered what they needed. Industrious and upbeat, they thanked the two Turks as they passed. The last person to leave drove a truck piled high with portable generators. He waved to them as he drove out the gate.

"Maybe Midgar has a future after all, huh?" said Reno.

"I'd like to believe that. C'mon, we've got work to do."

"Weapons and ammo, right?"

"Yeah. Plus, vehicles and fuel. And then we are changing all the access codes. The gate, the buildings, all of them."

As they worked late into the night, Tseng and Elena came to check on them. Even with their help, the job took until morning. They were grateful to get back to the company housing and catch some shut-eye, but they were awoken just a few hours later when Verdot barged in unannounced right before noon.

"Yikes. I'd be less freaked out if my dad woke me up," Reno remarked. "And he's dead."

"I find it more disturbing that the Turks of all people are sleeping in during a major crisis."

"I *meant* it's good to see you."

"..."

Verdot had no response for Reno's sincere grin. So instead he launched into a rundown of what he'd learned about Lieutenant Kylegate of the Junon forces.

"He was on leave in Kalm, but he gathered all the soldiers he could find and told them they were under his command. This morning, he held a rally to the east of Midgar and gave a speech about establishing a new city there. They had machinery that looked to be company property."

"Verdot— Sir," said Tseng, uncertain how to address the man who was technically no longer his commander. "That is all consistent with the intelligence we have. But I need to know something. In what capacity are you working, when you give us this information?"

"Why am I telling you, in other words." Verdot narrowed his eyes. "Let's just say I'm repaying a debt."

"We appreciate the assistance. But I'm not sure you owe us anything."

"Sheesh, what does it matter?" Reno broke in. "Why does he need some deep reason to help us out with intel? Y'know, you *are* allowed to just accept things without questioning them."

"I don't trust gifts," said Tseng flatly.

Verdot turned to him. "Reno. For me, the Turks are..."

Then he trailed off and swallowed the rest of the sentence. An awkward silence descended on the room.

Finally, Reno bowed his head like a contrite child and resumed the discussion.

"We saw volunteers carting construction equipment from the storehouses last night."

He was trying to sound especially businesslike, as if ashamed of his outburst.

"But something doesn't make sense. A lieutenant wouldn't have the clearance for those codes," said Rude.

"Right," said Verdot. Clearly, he'd already noted this. "The lieutenant was spending his leave in Kalm. And he had emergency access codes that he had no business knowing. Who gave them to him? And where was the president when he disappeared? Turks, you have yourselves a lead."

They jumped to their feet at once. Trying to hide his excitement, Tseng asked, "What else can you tell us about this Lieutenant Kylegate?"

Verdot shared everything he knew. Kylegate was born to an affluent family. He had already lost both parents and inherited everything. There was no need for someone of his means to enlist in military service, but he did, citing lofty goals such as destroying Shinra's enemies and establishing world peace. As a soldier, he was capable enough, but his superiors had expressed doubts on more than one occasion regarding his character.

"Brutal, sadistic tendencies, known for going too far in training and in the field. Talk in the barracks had it that the real reason he joined the military was so he could have a legal outlet for his...more unsavory appetites."

"Sounds like a real piece of work. Assuming he has the president, do you have any idea where he could be holding him?" said Tseng.

"My best guess would be Kalm. At the Kylegate villa."

Even as Verdot was finishing the sentence, Reno, Rude, and Elena were dashing from the room.

Then Reno turned back. "Where are the rest of the Turks? It'd feel better if we had more firepower."

"Scattered all over. On assignment, mostly. But also… Well, let's face it. Lots of people have their own worries now and got more to think about than their old jobs. I'm sure they came to Midgar out of duty just as I did, when Meteor was threatening us. But it's not in my power to command them anymore."

Reno was clearly unhappy with the answer. *They're still Turks, dammit.* But he left without saying anything.

"What are you going to do, sir?" Tseng paused to ask.

"Return to Junon. Reeve is headed there."

"That is…concerning."

"Agreed. If it were only Reeve's intentions I couldn't discern, that would be one thing, but there are others muddying the picture."

"You can trust the Turks. All of us who came that night. You taught us well, sir, and we still live by your lessons."

"Hah. Maybe that's why I can't guess what the lot of you are thinking." Verdot stepped past Tseng, exiting the room first.

"Find the president," he said.

Tseng watched him leave.

I was hoping you would send us off, sir. Like the old days.

Rufus was helpless to defend himself as Mütten Kylegate calmly punched him three times, hard.

"I can't tell you what I don't know."

"Give me the new access codes!"

"Someone else must have changed them. I only knew the emergency codes. How could I—?"

Mütten didn't wait for him to finish before hitting him again. He threw a mean punch. Combat trained.

"Military man, are you?"

"You've seen me plenty of times. But I guess us rank-and-filers are invisible to you."

"I'm sorry." Rufus meant it. But at the same time, he was turning Mütten's words over in his mind.

If this was a second home and it did in fact belong to Mütten, it meant he had money. Serious money, judging by the decor. It would be normal for a man of means to rise up the ranks quickly—and given his age, he should have gotten high enough by now for Rufus to have had dealings with him. Money wasn't supposed to speed up promotions, of course, but it did. The fact that Mütten wasn't at least a major meant something else had held him back. *Like, for example, his character. On which this weird room casts some serious doubt*, Rufus thought.

"You must have had underlings with you." Mütten unexpectedly changed the subject. *Underlings.* That classless word said a good deal about the man's worldview. "So where are they?"

"Good question. You grabbed me when my subordinates were away. I don't know where they are, and obviously, they don't know where I am."

"I see." Mütten seemed to accept that, but he drew back a fist to hit Rufus anyway. He was stopped only by a knock at the door.

"What is it?"

"Someone here to see you, sir," replied the housekeeper.

"To see me? Who the hell—? Never mind. Tell them I'm coming."

As he left, Mütten turned back to Rufus. "Construction of the new city began this morning. My underlings were there in force. We had volunteers, too. I'm told the crowds were massive. Hearing that was like music to my ears. Really, I can't wait, Mr. Shinra. This city will be the new capital of the planet—and *I'll* be the one who controls it. It's a pity you won't be around to see it."

The city would eventually be called Edge, and ironically, it would be Mütten who would never see it. Soon after he left the room, the sound of shouting came from upstairs. Rufus recognized the voice. Then there were gunshots, and the housekeeper screamed.

A few moments later, he heard the crackle of fire and smelled smoke. There were shouts and the sound of people running in a panic.

Rufus tried to stand up from the chair he'd been placed in, but he moved too quickly and fell down hard. His ribs sent sharp, jabbing pains through his body. Gritting his teeth against the pain, he scanned the room. Upstairs, it sounded like the fire was quickly becoming an inferno.

"Rufus Shinra! Where are you?!"

That was the same man who had held the shotgun on him in Kalm, Rufus was certain. Internal strife? A coup within the gang? Whatever was happening, he guessed this wasn't a rescue party looking for him.

So what to do? Under the bed. He could hide there. He started to crawl.

"Ungh."

The pain from his broken bones and the recent beating made his head spin, but he bit his lip and stifled a cry.

Eventually, he made it to the bed. But now what? They were bound to notice the chain running from the hook on the wall to his fetters under the bed. Rufus turned over on his back to look at the bed's underside. There were metal hooks here, which held several barbed whips. He tried not to think what they were for—or who they had been used on. He took one and tightened his fingers around the leather-wrapped handle.

"Shinra!" The man broke down the door with a tremendous crash. Rufus could see only his boots as he came closer to the bed. The man stood next to the chain and kicked it to test the tension.

"So there you are."

Closer. Come closer. Just as Rufus expected, the man was moving toward the bed. Now he was kneeling down. *That's right, down here. Take a peek.*

What appeared from above the bed, though, was not a face but the gleaming muzzle of a gun. Rufus instantly grabbed the barrel and twisted it upward, toward the underside of the bed.

"What the hell?!"

The gun fired, the recoil wrenching his hand. He released the barrel and rolled out from under the bed. The adrenaline had kicked in now, and the pain in his ribs was a distant scream he could ignore. Channeling his momentum, he slammed his cast-encased foot hard into a spot below the man's kneecap.

"Urgh!" the man groaned, staggering back. Rufus pulled himself upright and cracked the whip at him. It snagged the man's gun arm. He screamed and dropped the weapon.

Once again, luck was on Rufus's side. The gun fell within his reach. He stooped to pick it up and quickly trained the muzzle on his opponent.

"Game's over. Don't move."

Smoke was beginning to drift into the room.

"What're you gonna do, shoot me? Go ahead, Mr. President. Give it your best shot. But you'd better ask yourself how you're gonna get outta here, with those chains attachin' you to the wall. And do it quick, 'cause this place is burnin' fast."

The man was right. Rufus needed help to get the chains off. He had to keep talking, try to persuade the man.

"Did you kill Mütten?"

"Damn right I did. We grew up together, and he always treated me like shit."

"Seems to me like he had it coming."

"What, you're makin' like you're my pal, now? Shit. I haven't forgotten how you made me look bad in front of the guys."

So that's coming back to bite me, huh? Rufus thought. This was starting to look like mission impossible. *I was so damn close*, he thought.

Suddenly, there was another gunshot, and the man slumped to the floor, dead. As Rufus glanced down at the gun in his hand, wondering if he'd fired it by accident, more company arrived.

"*Boss!* You here?!"

The front yard of the Kylegate villa was thronged with Midgar refugees. The fire had started in the kitchen, and by the time the four Turks arrived, the villa was a burned-out husk with smoke still curling up from debris in the center.

"Excuse me."

They picked among the haggard refugees, giving Rufus's description and asking if they'd seen him. Eventually, they found a couple of witnesses willing to answer their questions.

"They're saying a man, maybe in his fifties, came out of the burning house carrying another man dressed in a white suit with a neck brace and a cast on his foot," Elena reported with a frown.

"That's got to be him," said Tseng.

"But who the hell was the other guy?" Reno asked.

"Time for more legwork," said Rude.

"Chief, about that." Reno squinted in distaste. "Havin' to be polite and everything is really slowing us down. Any chance we could use extra persuasion, Turk-style? I mean, everyone already hates Shinra anyway."

"Permission granted. But don't get rough with the construction volunteers."

"Why not them, specifically?"

"I have a feeling this whole project to build a new city came from the president himself."

In the basement of Mütten's burning mansion, a man who looked to be in his fifties pointed a gun at Rufus.

"Mr. Rufus Shinra. How are you today?"

It was the doctor who had checked his wounds previously.

"I've been better."

"You ought to put down the gun, then, before you get hurt even worse."

Rufus didn't much like the idea of giving up his weapon when the doctor was waving his own in his face.

"You're right, Doctor; guns are dangerous. Why don't we both put them down?"

The doctor smirked and adjusted his aim, right at Rufus's forehead. His trigger finger tensed. Rufus didn't hesitate. He aimed for the doctor's chest and pulled the trigger.

There was only an empty click.

"You overestimate the former owner of that gun, Mr. Shinra. He was Mütten's henchman and always had to do his boss's dirty work, but he never got any of the rewards for himself. He rather hated that. So when he finally got the chance to gun Mütten down, he nearly emptied the cartridge. I heard him fire the last shot down here. Or was that you?"

Looking at the dead man on the floor, Rufus sighed. *Not the type to think ahead, were you?*

"My name is Kilmister. In my younger days, I worked for the Shinra Company. I would like to claim I was an assistant to Dr. Hojo, but honestly, I barely saw the man. I was a lowly technician."

One of Hojo's staff members? Rufus had a bad feeling about this.

"Now, will you please put down the gun."

There was nothing for it but to toss the gun at Kilmister's feet.

Kilmister took a small glass phial from his pocket and held it out.

"I'd like you to take a whiff of this. It'll knock you out for a little while. If you refuse, I'll have to shoot you. Not to kill, because I want your cooperation—but it will hurt more than the chloroform."

Rufus took the proffered phial and removed the stopper. He remembered the smell—it was the same stuff Mütten had used to knock him out in the house in Kalm.

He awoke in the cargo bed of a truck with nine other people. Four men and five women, all in their early twenties, all listlessly hugging their knees. At first, Rufus thought they were covered in mud or oil, but when he looked closer, he could see that the black stains on their bodies were not dirt. The same dark, sticky fluid seeped out from under their hair. Some of them moaned intermittently. All of them looked to be in pain.

A young woman beside him toppled against him as the truck hit a bump.

"Sorry."

"It's all right."

"You're not sick, are you?" Her voice was hoarse with pain or perhaps exhaustion. "If you catch it…I'm sorry."

He had broken bones from his mad slide from the top of the Shinra Building. He had been chained up, beaten, and threatened with guns. And now he was going to contract some disease? Rufus could only smile drily to himself. Whatever the illness was, he really didn't need any more troubles, but stuck as he was in the back of this truck, there wasn't much he could do about it.

He could see Kilmister at the wheel, and despite the poor condition of the roads, he drove at a reckless speed, making the truck bounce as it went. Rufus considered jumping out, but he remembered that Kilmister wanted his cooperation. He could take that to mean that wherever they were going, he would be kept alive, for a while at least. Flinging himself from a fast-moving vehicle in the middle of nowhere, however, when he was already too injured to move far, seemed foolhardy, if not downright suicidal.

Kilmister stopped the truck near the coast, in front of a cave entrance partly hidden by rocky outcroppings. Rufus had been unconscious for the first part of the ride, so just as when he'd been taken to Mütten's basement, he had little idea how far they had traveled. But it was the coast, so according to his mental map, that should put them at least three or four hours' drive from the villa. A couple of days by foot, probably—for someone without busted ribs and feet.

Kilmister herded him at gunpoint, which was hardly necessary. He didn't have the strength to mount a resistance, and the others seemed happy to do what the doctor told them. The woman who had apologized during the ride helped Rufus down from the truck. Without crutches, he had to lean on her all the way into the cave.

"Well, here's hoping we both get better," she said.

Yes, that would be ideal, he thought.

*   *   *

The interior of the cave did not inspire much optimism.

After struggling down a ladder that leaned against a sixteen-foot-high rock face, Rufus twisted his neck against the brace to look back up. If the ladder was removed, there would be no way to climb out. And predictably enough, once all the people had made it down, Kilmister pulled away the ladder.

"The tunnels branch out into other tunnels, but they all lead to dead ends. Each of you can find a dead end you like. That will be your room."

"What about medical care? Are we getting any?" a man asked.

"Just come back here when you're told. I'll look after you." Kilmister's tone was placid, as if he were doing the rounds in a hospital. And with that, he was gone.

It turned out the cave was outfitted with simple hospital cots, clean sheets, and blankets, enough for everyone. The captives each picked a "room" and set up their beds there.

Rufus took the farthest dead end—predictable of him, always distancing himself. Later, a young man whose symptoms looked less severe than the others came around with a basic meal of bread, cheese, and water.

"Was anyone else forced to come here at gunpoint, or was it just me?" Rufus asked.

"Not that I know of. We've been patients of Dr. Kilmister since we were kids," said the young man. "He's the local doctor in Kalm, y'know. So when he said he thought he knew how to cure us, well, we didn't hesitate. In fact, me and some other folk came here earlier to bring the stuff for the hospital."

"You call this a hospital?"

"Sure. I know it's kind of a weird location, but we've gotta be under quarantine. He said people would chase us off if we stayed in town." He paused, looking troubled for a moment. "He said he had to use a gun on you 'cause you tried to run."

"It seems he does not trust all his patients equally," said Rufus. "Where are we anyway?"

"Sorry, but Dr. Kilmister said not to tell you."

So from one unknown hole in the ground to another. This excursion isn't getting much better, is it? Rufus thought.

At least Kilmister was willing to treat his wounds. The doctor had a rudimentary office set up near the bottom of the rock face by the entrance.

Kilmister changed Rufus's cast and brace, while the boy who handed out the food stood behind him, holding the gun.

"Are you making any progress treating the disease, Doctor?"

"Of course."

Rufus didn't miss the way Kilmister's glance flicked toward the boy.

"What are you trying to do here?"

"I'm a doctor, young man. I want to rid the world of sickness."

"That is an admirable goal. But what do you need me for?"

"Jenova."

"*What?*" That was just about the last thing he expected. Rufus couldn't hide his surprise.

"There are several similarities—on the cellular level, that is—between the people infected by the disease and the SOLDIER operatives I once worked on."

"Such as?" Rufus asked.

Kilmister glanced at the boy again. "All in due course."

He continued tending to Rufus in silence.

"Can you at least tell me if it's contagious?"

"I'll answer that soon, too."

So it isn't, Rufus thought.

Three months went by. Rufus no longer needed the brace, and Kilmister had finally removed the cast from his foot and given Rufus a makeshift cane instead.

"This is a metal pipe," said Rufus.

"Yes. From the wreckage inside the Shinra Building. We must make do in times like these," Kilmister informed him.

"How are things in Midgar?"

"The pox is the major problem. It appears to be claiming more and more people. Except, technically, no one's living in Midgar anymore. A new city is going up to the east. The people are building it themselves, for the most part."

Rufus thought of his grand vision that he'd partially shared with Mütten.

"Is anyone in charge of the project?"

"Apparently not. It appears to be a cooperative venture among several groups. By the by, Mr. Shinra, would you like to know what your company thugs are up to?"

Rufus guessed he meant the Turks. He nodded.

"It seems they have been threatening anyone who tries to access the company headquarters or the storehouses. Trespassers will be shot on sight, that sort of thing. It has scared people enough that hardly anyone ventures up to Sector Five or the Shinra Building."

Is that your doing, Tseng? Rufus couldn't quite keep himself from smiling.

"Now, at some point in the future, I am going to need to procure some equipment and materials that are currently in the company's possession. I'd appreciate it if you could talk to your thugs when the time comes."

"What do you need?" Rufus made himself sound indifferent, although he was anything but.

"Just some scientific equipment Dr. Hojo was using."

"Equipment you need to treat the disease, is that right?"

Kilmister smirked in a way that reminded Rufus of Hojo's unsettling smile. "Naturally. And I believe I mentioned this before, but—"

"Jenova."

"Yes. Where is she now?"

"I don't know. I might be able to find out, if you let me go, but stuck down here..." Rufus shrugged.

Kilmister fixed him with an appraising look. "Well, I'm going to need a new facility anyway. This place isn't properly set up for experiments."

Experiments?

"Are you a physician, Dr. Kilmister? Or a scientist?"

"I think we're done for today," said Kilmister, drawing a gun from inside his white lab coat.

After that, Rufus had plenty of time to work on his rehabilitation. The ribs were the slowest to heal, but eventually, he got to the point where he could move about freely inside the cave. He visited some of the other "rooms." Several were unoccupied. The young man who had been bringing him his meals was one of the first to go. Rufus now counted three men and two women; four of the patients had already died.

The woman who had helped him from the truck was still alive but in terrible agony. She was confined to her bed, and when Rufus came to her room, a man was with her, fretfully trying to offer comfort. He looked up when Rufus came in.

"The doctor said he's low on medicine, and he had to cut back on the dosage. I gave her my dose, but I think it's already worn off."

Rufus didn't see that there was anything he could do, but he had to try. He went to the foot of the rock face and called for Kilmister. At length, Kilmister appeared in his lab coat and looked down morosely.

"We're short on medicine here. One of the women—"

"My original stockpile is running low, and I haven't had any deliveries since you arrived. The rationing cannot be helped."

"*My* stockpile?" Since when had he been collecting this medicine? Since before the pox appeared? If so, why?

"Wait there," Kilmister said. He left and reappeared with the ladder. "Can you climb up?"

As he grasped the ladder, Rufus immediately began to consider the possibility of escape. He took each rung cautiously, but before he could climb onto the ledge above, Kilmister pointed the gun at him. "That's as far as you go. Stay there and listen to me."

Up close, Rufus could see beads of sweat on Kilmister's ashen face. "You don't look too hot, Doctor."

"I need medicine."

"For the patients?"

"For me."

Kilmister explained that he had been giving the patients a diluted form of a stimulant supplied to the Shinra military forces. "It can't do anything for the disease, but it does help with the pain."

"Is that your idea of a cure?"

"I'm not misleading them. I have to find the cause. Until I do, I can only treat the symptoms."

"Including your own? You have the disease?"

"No. Stimulants enable me to work through the night."

"And they make addicts of those who abuse them," Rufus said flatly. But even as he said it, he realized with a mild sense of triumph that he had discovered a means to control Kilmister. "Do you have a phone? Or at least pen and paper?"

"You want to send a message?"

"Yes. To my 'thugs,' as you call them. The Turks will know where to find more of the drug."

Rufus did not fail to notice the craving that flashed in Kilmister's eyes, but the doctor quickly hid it and coolly ordered Rufus to climb back down. Still, only a few minutes passed before he tossed down a pen and some paper.

Rufus wrote out a request to procure the stimulant and nothing more. His job was to gain Kilmister's trust. The Turks would handle the rest.

Kilmister left for Midgar that day. He told Rufus he would go to the Shinra Building, find the Turks, and give them the note. That should have taken three days, tops, but he didn't return on the third day, or the fourth, or the fifth. The Turks didn't come, either. Rufus had assumed they would trail Kilmister to the cave and effect a rescue. Instead, a week passed with no visitors. Their supply of food was dwindling.

Rufus wandered the cave—he knew every nook and cranny by now—in an attempt to make the long empty hours pass more quickly. The woman who was confined to bed was growing weaker. She barely seemed lucid. The man looking after her still sat with her, but he also let out muffled groans as he clutched her hand tight and waited for a miracle.

"Kilmister will be back soon," Rufus told them—an entirely baseless statement, practically a lie. After the words were out, he wondered what could have prompted him to say it.

The disaster came suddenly. For some time, they had heard the heavy rain outside, muffled as the sound was, but no one suspected that the cave might flood. The water came in not from the direction of the entrance but from the dead end that Rufus had claimed as his room. The ceiling was full of holes, which suddenly turned into so many faucets.

This couldn't be the first time it had rained since they came here. Why was this happening now? Perhaps it was a particularly heavy rainfall, and a natural reservoir somewhere was overflowing. Whatever the cause, the water level was rising quickly, and they had to find a way out. He headed for the rock face at the entrance, shouting out warnings down the pathways leading to the other dead ends.

His injured neck still protested as he peered up the sheer wall, but of course he could see no one. The only sound was the distant pummeling of the rain. Rufus scanned the area. If the water pouring in from the back of the cave filled this area, eventually they would be buoyed up to the top of the wall. Assuming everyone could manage to stay afloat that long.

What choice do we have?

He ran back and informed the others that they needed to prepare to evacuate. But after a week without the stimulant that served as an analgesic, they were in too much pain to reply.

"Five people...," he muttered, then committed himself to a course of action. He went to the farthest occupied room first and carried its occupant toward the entrance. The man had lost enough weight to be distressingly light, but that meant even in his own weakened state, Rufus was able to move him. Then he went back for the rest.

The water was already rising past his ankles. He looked for items that might help them stay above the water. A few of the wooden bed frames were beginning to float. They were cheaply made, held together by removable metal fittings, so he dismantled one and pushed the pieces toward the entrance. The water bore them away down the passage.

"If you can swim, swim," said Rufus. "If you can't, grab hold of these. One for each person."

In a few hours, the water was up to his chin. Some of the others were already bobbing in the water, clinging to the pieces of wood. Rufus had done what he could, and now there was nothing for it but to gaze up at the ledge above them and wait. Finally, he too had to grab a piece of wood to stay above water.

Time passed, and the water level continued to rise. The patients floated closer and closer to the ledge, until it was almost within arm's reach. But then the water stopped rising. Either the rain had subsided, or an outflow had been reached somewhere else in the cave system. Rufus pursed his lips in frustration. They had nowhere to go. Their only hope was rescue from outside.

They took stock and did a head count, and they found only two men and one woman remained; the woman was the same one who had helped him from the truck, all those weeks ago. The man who cared for her had bundled two pieces of wood together so she could lie down. Just as Rufus wondered if she was still alive, her face twisted with a spasm of pain.

Somehow, seeing that was a relief.

Hours crawled by, and nothing changed. The water level stayed the same. Submerged in the chilly waters, they were losing body heat. It occurred to Rufus that they wouldn't last much longer.

"What?" He thought someone had spoken to him, but no one had the strength to speak. He peered around himself groggily. Something was creeping along the surface of the water—something black. It slowly floated toward him. He thought it must be the viscous fluid that seeped from the disease's victims.

No, that can't be right. It was moving like something with a will of its own. Fear took hold of Rufus. He splashed uselessly at the water, trying to push away the encroaching black shadow, but the waves he made had no effect on it. He looked on in horror as the stuff closed in around him and soaked his white suit with inky stains.

Not that the suit was really white by this point. He had insisted on wearing it each day, in case a chance to escape presented itself. *Escape, hah!* Now, as he watched the cuffs turn black, for the first time since he had been kidnapped, he thought: *I'm going to die.*

The black stuff seemed to crawl up his neck and onto his face. It was trying to get into his mouth. He kept his lips clamped shut. So it went for his nostrils, and he pinched his nose. That left him with no way to breathe, but suffocating would be a better way to go. Still, it didn't stop—it was in his *ears*—

As long as I don't scream, he thought as everything went dark.

"Mr. Shinra? Mr. Shinra!"

Rufus opened his eyes.

"Damn this flood. I did not anticipate this. Sorry for the delay." Kilmister was plunging the ladder down into the water.

Somewhat surprised to find himself alive, Rufus reached out and took hold of a rung. As for the others, he saw the woman from the truck and the man who'd nursed her, clinging to the pieces of wood. The others were gone.

"Are you two all right?"

The man lifted his head.

"Help's finally arrived," Rufus added.

The man stared at Rufus in a daze, then remembered what was happening and frantically called to the woman. She responded with a faint movement of her head.

Rufus stretched his hand out to her—and then there was a gunshot from above.

The woman drifted back from the wooden float as if shoved and silently sank beneath the water.

"*Pamela!*" the man cried. He let go of the float to dive after her, but he was too weak to swim. Rufus took the float and moved toward him, grabbing his arm.

"Pamela!" he was shouting in anguish, but he had no more strength.

Pulling him along, Rufus swam back to the ladder. "Climb."

"But—"

"Just concentrate on staying alive."

The man stared at the dark, empty water that had swallowed up Pamela. Rufus realized he had only just now learned her name.

Finally, the man looked up to glare at Kilmister in seething rage.

"There was nothing we could have done for her. It was an act of mercy. Pamela would thank me, if she could."

It's not Pamela's forgiveness you ought to worry about, Rufus thought. Hatred was settling into the man's face as he began to climb the ladder.

"What's your name?" Rufus asked.

"Judd."

"Listen, Judd. Don't do anything yet. I'll handle Kilmister."

Judd made no reply and kept climbing. Rufus followed after him. Just as he was about to reach the top—solid ground, at long last—an excruciating pain seized his entire body. He felt something drip from the corner of his mouth.

He wiped his face to find that same dark slime on his hand, just like Pamela and Judd.

"Well, well, Mr. President. It looks like you'll be needing some of the drug yourself." Kilmister sounded inordinately pleased. *"—Urk!"*

That yelp also came from the doctor. The gun fell from his hand and into the water.

Gritting his teeth against the pain, Rufus looked up to see Kilmister's face contorted in a struggle. Someone had him in a choke hold from behind. *Damn it, Judd. I said not now.*

"Ghk…"

But then he realized Judd was sitting on the ledge, head bowed and groaning. Fighting to keep his grip on the ladder as relief washed over him, he summoned all his remaining strength for a furious shout. *"What in blazes took you so long?!"*

"Sorry, Boss!"

Back in its early days, before the company had grown to its full might, the Shinra Electric Power Company had built a mountain resort as an R and R facility for employees. But most people preferred the beach to the mountains, and the resort soon fell into disuse. Indeed, there were several lodges that had sat untouched since they were built.

The seven of them—Rufus, Tseng, Elena, Reno, Rude, Kilmister, and

Judd—made the trip in two vehicles. When they arrived at the resort, it was already full of disease victims. The majority were Kilmister's patients, brought from Kalm by the Turks. As Rufus cast a dubious look around him, Tseng started to explain.

A week ago, Kilmister had appeared in the Shinra Building, demanding to talk to the Turks. Reno and Rude, who were detailed to monitor the building, heard the man saying he had a letter from Rufus Shinra. At the prospect of obtaining information on their missing president, they promptly left their stakeout spot and approached him and asked for the letter.

Provide all available stock of military-issue stimulant to the doctor bearing this note.

It seemed awfully random, not to mention suspicious, and they doubted it had really come from Rufus. They told Kilmister to come back the next day. Reno trailed him while Rude went straight to their makeshift office in Sector Five to report to Tseng.

Tseng thought it looked like Rufus's handwriting and signature, but he couldn't be certain. But it was the best lead they had had in a long time, so they decided to give Kilmister what he asked and then follow him.

Meanwhile, Reno trailed Kilmister to Kalm. The doctor had a small clinic there, but because he had not been there in some time, it had been taken over by refugees in need of shelter. The refugees were delighted at Kilmister's return, and they clamored at him for treatment and medicine. When Reno peeked in the window, Kilmister appeared to be in a foul mood as he reluctantly dealt with his patients. The doctor was no picture of health himself, in fact.

The next day, in the main lobby of the Shinra Building, the Turks handed over several cases of the stimulant. Kilmister immediately ripped open one of them, twisted the cap from a bottle, diluted the contents with water, and chugged the concoction. Then, ignoring the nonplussed stares of the Turks, he stretched himself out on the floor and told them he was going to rest right there until the drug took effect.

The Turks fumed at the man's arrogance and gritted their teeth against their own impatience. But he was their only lead to finding the president. If he said wait, then wait they must.

Finally, his mood and complexion much improved, Kilmister lurched to his feet and ordered the Turks to carry the cases down to the surface.

Clearly feeling in control, he asked whether Tseng might know of an appropriate location where he could house a large number of patients. Somewhere remote but not *too* difficult to access.

"If I am to do my part for the world, I need the proper facilities," said Kilmister.

Perhaps sensing he was pushing too hard, he then talked about the president, describing his status in detail and accurately enumerating all the injuries Rufus had suffered. The Turks had to take him at his word.

"I was the one who saved him from the fire at Mütten's house. I've been treating him ever since," Kilmister added. "He'd be dead without me. I hope that the company understands it is in my debt."

When they asked why he hadn't bothered to tell anyone until now, he laughed and said he first needed the young president to see things his way.

Tseng immediately thought of the mountain resort as a location for Kilmister's facility. After they took him to see it, the doctor gave it his seal of approval and demanded that those afflicted with the disease be brought there. The Turks balked at taking orders from this drug-addicted nobody, but he reminded them that until his facility was ready, he would not be inclined to tell them where the president was. They had no choice but to obey.

The Turks lost track of how many trips they made between Kalm and the resort, ferrying patients and equipment. But finally, satisfied that the Turks had done his bidding, Kilmister said he would take them to their president.

On the way, the flooded roads caused the Turks to lose sight of Kilmister's truck.

"But I found the cave anyway, with my secret agent's intuition!" declared Reno, hoping the fact would make up for losing the doctor in the first place and being late to reach the cave.

Rufus stayed at the mountain resort, too, as one of the patients. They could treat only some of the symptoms, not the disease itself, but the diluted stimulant did help with the pain. The Turks attended to him in shifts, and if the fever was down and he felt well enough, they would brief him on the latest intelligence so that he might consider the next step.

"In this new city, do they have a city center? Have they built anything there?" he asked Reno one day, after something occurred to him.

"Uh...the plaza, I guess. Just an open, circular area. Looks pretty much like the whole city grew around it, though. It's on that main road out of Midgar, too. So, yeah, it's kinda the center of town, I'd say."

"Then we should put something there," Rufus mused. "A monument."

"A monument to what?"

"Officially, to the planet fighting off Meteor."

"Officially? So what would it be unofficially?"

"A symbol of ownership. *Our* ownership."

"Claiming the center of town for Shinra? I like it."

People still blamed Shinra for the disaster, but the company was regaining a measure of trust by providing materials, equipment, fuel, and medicine. Reeve, the former director of urban planning, sent heavy machinery and manpower from Junon. By now, it was clear that Reeve was no ally of the company, but as long as the Turks—and Verdot's group of former Turks—were acting for the common good, he did nothing to interfere with their operations.

With the help of volunteers, Reno began construction of the monument. Those who wanted to see something meaningful in the plaza were glad to be a part of the project. Although some balked, loudly, when they learned that Shinra was behind it, Reno defused the potential crisis with typical Turk methods.

The number of patients at the mountain resort changed continually, but for a while, it truly felt like a refuge, free from the troubles of the outside world.

Soon enough, however, a crisis arose. It began when Kilmister started protesting that the stimulant was being used too quickly and would soon run out.

Elena, who spent a lot of time in the new city, had suggested they distribute the medicine to people there as well, and Rufus had approved. But inevitably, this drained their supplies much faster than planned, and now there were hardly any reserves left in the storehouses. Rufus ordered the Turks to find people with pharmaceutical expertise who could set up a manufacturing operation for the stimulant. They could use the company facilities, he suggested, and also contact Reeve for assistance if necessary.

It was not enough for Kilmister. He demanded that their first priority was to secure enough of the existing reserves to keep the mountain resort supplied. Tseng and the others sneered, knowing the drug-addicted doctor's motives were entirely selfish, but Rufus himself was strangely willing to indulge the doctor.

The stimulant's key ingredient was derived from the tail of the Nibi bear. Because the ingredient would be highly diluted, a single tail could provide enough to manufacture a large quantity of the drug.

It fell to Elena to find a steady source of the raw material.

"Hey, Rude?" Reno was frowning, which he didn't do often. "Why's the boss putting up with Kilmister's crap?"

"I guess he's hoping the research into a cure will pan out eventually." He shrugged.

"What research? Any moron can hand out painkillers. I sure could," Reno scoffed.

"He's doing more than that. He took a tissue sample from me a while back. Said it was as a control. Who knows? Maybe he'll have a breakthrough."

"He can take a sample out of me, too. I don't have it, either. Come to think of it, it's kinda weird that we're surrounded by patients all the time and we never get it. What's the deal?"

"The president said it's not contagious."

Reno still looked unconvinced. Rude crouched into a boxer's stance and punched Reno in the shoulder, half-strength.

"How about a sparring session? It's been a while since the last one."

"What, now?"

"Yeah. Get your body moving, clear your mind. Maybe we don't get sick 'cause we're in shape. C'mon. You don't want to go soft, do you?"

"Sheesh. You sound like my old boxing coach."

But Reno was smiling as he crouched into his own fighting stance.

All right, he thought. *Let's do this!*

The cabal. This was what the other patients at the mountain resort called Rufus and his tight-knit group of henchmen. Company solidarity was one thing, someone remarked, but this was on another level.

Even though the old company was essentially no more, the president and his subordinates still organized themselves according to that now-irrelevant hierarchy. It was natural to them, but to others, they seemed like they were children playing "office."

If it was a game, they played it with fervor and intensity. Indeed, they played like schoolkids lost in their make-believe, like kids who had only one another and no other place to call home.

One night, nearly two years after the chosen day, Rufus went to see Kilmister.

"So, Doctor. I think it's time you told us if your research is bearing any fruit. Have you made progress? What about the connection between the disease and Jenova?"

"You want to know about progress? All right, fine. I'm no closer to a cure now than I was two years ago. No progress at all. Zip."

Hopped up as usual on the stimulant, Kilmister spoke excitedly, as if delivering the long-awaited punch line to a joke. Rufus watched him, his expression neutral.

"However, I am starting to figure out the pathology behind it."

The first people to contract the disease were those directly exposed to the Lifestream. He had discovered this in the early stages of his research through interviewing patients, Kilmister explained smugly.

"The others, whose symptoms appeared later, had something else in common. They were suffering severe emotional distress. In almost all cases, they had lost a loved one or had a near-death experience of their own, and they had gone through a period of intense contemplation of death. I surmise you were no exception, Mr. Shinra?"

Rufus nodded. He remembered the cave, the water, the realization he was about to die.

"In the aftermath of the disaster, many people were fearful about the future, feeling a sense of impending doom. So the disease quickly became a pandemic."

The doctor paused.

"And then…there is the black liquid."

Rufus recalled that stuff in the flooded cave, flowing with sentient purpose along the surface of the water.

"Many of the patients who fell sick at a later time remember seeing black water. Those who noticed nothing out of the ordinary likely came into contact with it via contaminated water, without their knowledge. It can spread anywhere it wants, you see."

"What do you mean, it *wants*?" Rufus didn't like the implication in Kilmister's choice of words.

"The pain, the fever—these are signs that the body is fighting off a contaminating substance. It does appear that the black liquid is our true opponent."

"But what is it, exactly? Are you implying it has intent?"

"I believe it is related to Sephiroth's or Jenova's genetic material. But not the material itself. Perhaps I should call it a remnant—a memetic legacy? As I said before, the characteristics are very similar to what we observed in the SOLDIER program."

Rufus tensed at the name Sephiroth. He could remember an image of Sephiroth surfacing in his mind, for no apparent reason, when the black water surrounded him.

"Mr. Shinra, I want to focus my research on Jenova. But I need a sample. Where can I find the creature?" said Kilmister, oblivious to Rufus's alarm.

"I have no idea."

"Would you have your agents search for it?"

"I'll consider it."

"You do that. But don't take too long."

Rufus nodded and turned to leave. But Kilmister was in a talkative mood. *Must have taken more than usual,* thought Rufus.

"A long time ago, Dr. Hojo nixed a project I proposed. But the thought that it's not too late, that I could try it *now*—oh, it's just thrilling. I could create something even more powerful than Sephiroth; I just know it."

"I thought this was about finding a cure," Rufus said pointedly, without looking at him.

"Oh, I doubt we'll ever help the patients already exhibiting symptoms. And if those still in good health can keep from brooding over the future and their own death, they'll be all right. You can publicize that, by the way. Issue a public health warning. But not the part about the water. Not unless you want panic and riots on your hands."

Rufus, who was one of those people "exhibiting symptoms," left the room without another word.

The next morning, they found Kilmister dead from a gunshot wound. The man named Judd confessed immediately to Tseng.

"Where did you get the gun?" asked Tseng.

"I can't tell you that, sir. Not that I was told to keep quiet—but, well, it was a favor from a friend."

*　　*　　*

When Tseng reported Kilmister's murder and Judd's confession, Rufus's reaction was muted.

"Is that so?" he said idly, then dismissed the matter. "Tseng, I need your help."

"Sir."

"Shinra needs to find and secure any remaining genetic material from Jenova."

"...Yes, sir."

"We need to keep it out of other people's hands. That includes mad scientists." Rufus thought about what Kilmister had told him. "Or even ghosts lurking in the Lifestream."

If Tseng was confused, he didn't show it.

"Yes, sir. We'll prepare for the mission immediately."

Reno and Rude were repainting the sign outside the mountain resort.

"'Healen Lodge'? Is that what they're calling it?" said Reno, peering at the design. "What kind of a name is that?"

"One that gets the point across—that we're going to heal the world."

The partners turned with a start, caught unawares by Rufus standing behind them.

"Well, we might have to knock a few heads together to do it—but this is the Shinra Electric Power Company, after all. That shouldn't surprise anyone."

There was a spark in his voice, bright and alive.

She tried to think of some way to warn Cloud. As she pondered the problem, all the other things she couldn't tell him rose anew in her spirit, vivid as life. There was always so much she wanted to tell him. But she never had known what to say or how. She hadn't troubled herself over this for a long time, and eventually, she decided there was no point in thinking about it now, either, unless she found a way to talk to him.

She realized the one responsible for sowing all that hatred was trying to manifest himself in the living world. How was he going to do that? She mustered her courage and went to see for herself. He sensed her and gave chase, but then soon stopped. She could feel his mocking laughter behind her as she fled.

There is nothing you can do.

Still, she had seen what she needed to see—a glimpse of his intentions. He would begin by using others to act where he could not. Should she do the same? *No*, she thought. *Even if that's possible, I don't want to appear before Cloud as someone else. I want him to see me as he knows me.*